Here
with the
Winter

J. Penrod Scott

ARCHWAY
PUBLISHING

This is a work of fiction. All of the characters, names, incidents, organizations, and dialogue in this novel are either the products of the author's imagination or are used fictitiously.

Archway Publishing books may be ordered through booksellers or by contacting:

Archway Publishing
1663 Liberty Drive
Bloomington, IN 47403
www.archwaypublishing.com
844-669-3957

Cover Design by
Leslie J. Farinacci
Sketch by J. Penrod Scott

1 John 1:3

ISBN: 978-1-6657-0523-3 (sc)
ISBN: 978-1-6657-0524-0 (e)

Library of Congress Control Number: 2021906691

Print information available on the last page.

Archway Publishing rev. date: 05/12/2021

CHAPTER 1

Listen over the map. Listen over all the squares and roads and farms of Clover Township, Ohio, where over time families met and married each other and were somehow all related by land. Listen to all the voices rising up over the map of lanes and names of thirty-six square miles and over Grovewood Road, where a car was moving north, northeast ...

"Did you hear that Jessie Conrad is coming back?" Emmette Schiller III asked in the township's village of West Emmette, so named by his great-grandfather.

"Yeah," Burt Brown said back to his friend, leaning on a new Corvair parked at Emmette's gas station. "Nice she's coming back home." He nodded, his squint fixed steadily on his barbershop across the street. "Still can't believe Matthew's gone."

"What house is she going to? Henry's?"

"Nah. I heard she's movin' into Raymond's duplex," Burt said.

Local deputy Raymond Jones pulled into the station just then, parked his patrol car, and walked up to the two men. "Who are you talkin' about?"

"Jessie Conrad," they both answered.

"Oh yeah," he said slowly, removing his hat.

Burt took a packet of tobacco from his flannel shirt pocket. "Darn sad for those kids." He lit his pipe.

"At least they have Jessie," Emmette said.

"And their grandfather," Raymond added quietly.

"She movin' into your duplex?" Emmette asked Raymond.

"No," he said. "I told her she could live with us, in the other side of the house, until the check came in, but Bill told her she could move into 147. On Meadow. He just finished it."

"I heard Henry lost a little bit of money from the Pirates game," Emmette said.

"Didn't everyone?" Burt said with a quick exhale.

"Well, let's hope not too much," Raymond said, moving to the door of his car. "See you guys later." He stepped into the old sedan, tipping his cap to his friends, and brushing his chin with the stiff sleeve of his jacket.

The new residential street named Meadow Drive had been cut just three years before by the Zimmer brothers, who came to town ten years ago and bought farmland to create streets and houses for the tide of mill workers coming to the region. They were wise to do so, since families were attracted to the pastoral, rural village with its carousel of churches, rolling green acres, farms and dairies, penned history, and now the Zimmers' six new streets with two- and three-bedroom ranches. The Zimmer brothers' hammers hadn't cooled for a decade, and they would continue to staple time for another ten years over section eleven of the township, changing lots and lines on the yellowed plat of West Emmette.

Jessie Conrad had decided to come home after establishing an address in Columbus with her husband Matthew and their young son and daughter. They had even built a new house there, though it hadn't been finished when the accident happened. Now widowed, she continued in her determined drive beyond Grovewood Road and was approaching Main Street in West Emmette.

The town's Main Street, a length of one mile through the core of the village, was a shaded section of a historical thoroughfare and resting place for travelers journeying into Ohio from Western Pennsylvania. Jessie's father, Henry Marshall Hall, had owned and operated the flour mill there years before, and he still lived across the street from the property, in the very center of town. When Jessie was a girl, the village had three hundred residents. Today, in 1960, there were more than five hundred.

Jessie turned onto Meadow Drive, which formed a sort of blacktop river in its gentle new address. Houses on half- and three-quarter-acre lots faced each other with brand-new driveways still being purchased and poured. The street's lower half was flat and straight after a sharp bend inward from Main Street. From there, midway, the street sloped upward, turning up a gentle roll of land, formerly farmland, in a bend to the right and then a bend to the left. There, at the top, the slope leaned back flat into a crossroad, stop sign, and orchard. Up, up toward the top, past the new houses and some still-vacant lots, Jessie drove her husband's large car, with her two children peering intently out the windows at their mother's hometown.

Slowly Jessie pulled the Pontiac into a narrow gravel driveway on the left at the top of Meadow Drive. She brought the car to a stop in front of the garage door and turned off the engine. She wasn't used to driving such a distance—more than two hours from their former home. Relieved, Jessie took a deep breath and relaxed her tight grip on the steering wheel, her black nylon gloves stuck in clench to the mission. It was a crisp, cold December morning.

"There. Here we are. We can get out now," Jessie said to Charles and Charlotte in the back seat.

But Charles was already opening his car door. A baseball glove was on his hand, and he stepped out onto the gravel driveway, looking up, as if looking for a ball to fall from somewhere. It would soon enough.

Charlotte looked straight ahead to the house before her. Jessie knew her daughter wanted only to see her new room.

A blue doll trunk was next to Charlotte in the car, and she grabbed the top handle and swiftly swung it out of the car door with her. She carried her doll trunk across the gravel and stepped carefully over some uneven larger stones, heading into the side garage door Jessie had opened for her.

Inside the garage, the family of three stepped up two wooden stairs and into the house's kitchen. Once again there was the smell of fresh wall plaster and paint. Jessie stood in front of her children, holding the door. Facing them, she held her left arm outward, leading her children into their new home.

The woman felt relief, pride, worry, and grief all in that one gesture. Her petite hands would see much work to come. Her mind had already begun the exercise of making decisions alone. Her room would be ... her room alone.

"Which room is mine?" Charlotte called, hurrying through the house and down the hall, feeling excitement. The hall was the only way to go beyond the kitchen, dinette, and front room. Her head turned wildly. She peered into a small, longish room on the right. It had two windows on the back side of the house. Charlotte flung open a tall closed door at the end of the hall; it was a narrow closet of shelves. To the left was a bright room in the corner.

Jessie called back to her daughter, "Your room is next to that one! Next to mine, Charlotte. The other door on the left!"

Jessie watched as Charlotte disappeared into the square open room. The space had wooden floors like the other bedrooms, living room, and hall. That familiar, sharp smell of new plaster filled Charlotte's small nose. She quickly closed her bedroom door, slid open one of the double closet doors to her side, and set the blue doll trunk in its new place. Charlotte sat down inside the closet too, staring at the trunk. She opened its latch, took out her Terri Lee doll, and straightened the heavy, blonde silk hair with her small fingers, making certain the pink engagement ring was still in the trunk in Terri's black patent leather shoe.

Charles threw open his sister's bedroom door. "Where are you? Hey, Charlotte, look at this! Where are you?" He found her in the closet. "Come look at this!"

The brother and sister had shared a bedroom together at their former home. Charlotte peered out, clutching Terri Lee. "Charles, do you think there are ghosts here?"

"In a new house? Come on! No way! Geez. Now come and look!" He grabbed his sister's hand and pulled her up and out of the closet, down the hall, and back through the kitchen with a swift stride, Charlotte trying desperately not to trip. Charles slowed down at the basement stairwell and guided his young sister more carefully down the plank steps to a mass of fresh, gray, cured concrete.

"Look!" Charles shouted. "We can roller-skate down here! Get your skates!"

"Mine are in a box somewhere," Charlotte said, a smile slowly stretching her cheeks. Her eyes beheld the future possibilities of this big concrete room, with vertical green poles to climb and a dark-green beam running the ceiling length. It was very cold.

"Well, I have mine in the trunk. Mom!" Charles bolted up the stairs, threw open the back door, and ran to the Pontiac.

But just then, the moving truck and the two cars of his aunts and uncles arrived.

Jessie stepped outside. The appearance of the Conrad cars together again was unsettling, reminding both Jessie and her son of that day in October when Charles and Charlotte had walked home from school with their friend Walter in Columbus to find those cars parked in their driveway upon news of her husband's accident. Now, just two months later, their furniture and all their belongings were in a truck. Matthew's brother, Gordon, was driving it.

Gordon's wife, Margaret, stepped out of the first car. "Gosh, Jessie, your front yard is bare," she said to her sister-in-law. "Look how they left it. All those rocks …"

Matthew's sister, Nelle, emerged from the second car and took Jessie's arm. "The four of us will come in the spring and help you rake this, Jessie. Don't worry. We'll get your boxes and furniture inside, and you get ready for Christmas. This is lovely. Snow is in the forecast. This yard will be covered up for a while. Come on, let us see your kitchen."

Margaret's son, Will, also got out of the first car and tossed a football to his cousin Charles. Margaret bade Will not to turn an ankle on the uneven yard. "Watch your trousers! You need to wear those to school Monday!"

Nelle reached for a wrapped package in their car's front seat and carried it into the house, linking an arm with Jessie, while Nelle's husband, Howard, and brother, Gordon, flung open the rental truck doors.

"Margaret and I got a little gift for your new kitchen, Jessie," Nelle said. Charlotte followed the women.

The kitchen window over the sink was a double-hung window, as were all the windows of the house—and of all the houses on the street—except for a picture window in the living room at the front. The kitchen floor was brown- and orange-speckled linoleum. The Formica countertop ran across the kitchen's back wall and turned into a small island, a divider defining the kitchen from the dining space, anchored by two more vertical windows. Nelle looked up. "Ah yes, there is a plug."

Jessie loosened the wrapping paper and took out an oval, plastic, yellow kitchen clock for above the sink. It had a yellow gingham design behind the black, plastic clock hands. "Good. That should fit just fine enough," Nelle said, hugging Jessie in a comforting and encouraging way. She was soft spoken and had the face of a china doll but with eyes like Matthew's. Nelle and her husband, Howard, lived an hour's drive west, and the women hadn't had much chance to spend time together since high school and marriage other than holidays, but Jessie and Nelle liked each other very much.

Nelle had learned the news of her brother's truck accident when it was told on the radio that October morning two months ago. She had been sitting at her kitchen table and couldn't believe what she heard. She ran to the phone, then to the car to drive frantically to Columbus.

Margaret, married to Matthew's brother, Gordon, lived just twenty minutes from West Emmette. She said to Jessie while glancing at Charlotte, who was standing between them, "Where *did* she get this blonde hair?" Margaret pulled up a lock in question with a frown of disapproval. "Have you enrolled Charles and Charlotte in the grade school here yet?" Her own children attended school in Benton, a larger and financially stronger school system. "Do you want me to call Ohio Bell for a phone?"

"I have talked to the school office, and they are expecting us on Monday," Jessie replied, moving Charlotte gently by the shoulders to stand in front of her, giving her a small hug. "And a phone is coming on Tuesday. Thank you though."

Margaret went back outside to help the men, and Charlotte went to her room. In the kitchen, still empty and not yet christened with cooking aromas, Jessie pulled Nelle aside. "Wait here a moment, Nelle," and she reached for her purse. "This arrived in the mail just before we left Columbus." Jessie lifted an envelope from the purse. "Look at this," she whispered to her sister-in-law, pulling forth a photograph.

It was an elementary school group portrait of Charles's class in Columbus. "This was taken October twelfth." Jessie pointed to Charles, who stood in the back row. "Look," she whispered again, her voice desperate. "Just two days later he was thrown into a different life. And now here we are."

Jessie looked at the photograph. Nelle placed an arm around her friend's shoulder while Jessie, trembling a little, slid the photo back into the manila envelope sent from the school. "He still had a father that day, Nelle," Jessie said. "The boy in that photo still had a dad. And now he doesn't."

"Oh, Jess," Nelle whispered, tilting her head to touch Jessie's. "We'll help you. Don't worry."

Just then the back door flew open, and Charles was backing up the two garage steps with a nightstand. Will carried the other side. Jessie, lowering her head in acceptance, smiled rigidly and with a stiff hand put the envelope back in her purse. The women began the task of placing the simple furniture.

From their kitchen window next door, Gloria Walker and her son watched the activity and the new neighbors' arrival. The Lutheran church bells chimed the hour from Main Street, ringing twelve long peels; then those bells sent the lovely notes of the hymn "A Mighty Fortress Is Our God" dancing up into the air over the small, old town and new residents of West Emmette.

❊ ❊ ❊

"Let's say our prayers," Jessie said to Charles and Charlotte in Charlotte's room that night at bedtime. The three knelt at Charlotte's newly put-together bed and grasped their hands together in Jessie's two small fists on the family quilt. The beds had been assembled and some clothes hung, but all else was still in boxes. "Now I lay me down to sleep," Jessie began.

"Why does everyone care if we go back to school at all?" Charlotte interrupted.

Jessie turned a lock of hair from above her daughter's eye. "Well, believe me, Charlotte, you are going to like your new school here." Through the window the constellation Orion stretched across the sky, and the winter moon illumined the Conrads' empty back porch. "Trust me," Jessie added, quietly admiring the stars and moon. She clasped Charlotte's hand again. "Let's start over."

"Now I lay me down to sleep," they prayed together aloud. "I pray the Lord my soul to keep. If I should die before I wake, I pray the Lord my soul to take."

Charles, uneasy now with that old prayer of theirs, said good night and went over to his new room across the hall.

Charlotte crawled into her bed. "Leave the door open, Mommy," she said as Jessie pulled the soft, worn quilt gently up to her little girl's chin.

"I know," Jessie replied, kissing her forehead. "I will."

After turning off the room light and leaving the door ajar, Jessie walked down the hallway and into the front room to turn off the lamp sitting atop one of the moving cartons. The smell of hot dogs lingered, she noticed. Gordon had brought a little charcoal grill and left it for them. The temperature had reached forty degrees, and it had been fun for the family to grill in the backyard in December during a break in their move-in task. Margaret had even brought marshmallows.

Five cartons were stacked in the corner near the front door. Jessie opened one and looked inside. It held the family portrait, taken four years ago in Columbus, not long after their transfer there. Such a beautiful black-and-white portrait of the four of them. Matthew had purchased a small bow tie for Charles to match his own.

Jessie held the frame a minute, then set it back in the box. She looked about the room. There would be no place to set the mantel clock Matthew had made. Its delicate, black, iron scrolled hands pointed at 6:25, where they had stopped when the clock was unplugged for packing.

The green couch fit nicely against the back wall, she thought. There was Matthew's oak floor lamp and end table, where he had kept his ashtray. The glass-top coffee table her father had given them. The hi-fi cabinet. Matthew's chair. Her chair.

If fear swelled in Jessie's throat and chest that night, the children didn't know it. Jessie spotted her alarm clock in the box and carried it with her to turn off the kitchen light. She could hear a wind arriving, and she heard the new furnace click on below in the basement. It made a comforting, bass rolling exhale. The wind grew louder as clouds rushed more quickly into the night sky.

❄ ❄ ❄

Charlotte listened to her mother's footsteps move back down the hallway and into the bathroom. She could hear water running and a drawer open and close. A few minutes passed; then she heard her mother walk past her doorway, go into the corner bedroom, and turn off the bed lamp.

Charlotte pulled the covers up over her head, sat up, and turned on her flashlight. She opened the pages of her *Jolly Jingle Book*, given to her by her kindergarten teacher back home in June at the end of her first school year. There in the pages were the pictures of an elephant, a puppy, a cow, and the words she had looked at while holding the book in her father's arms. He had read them so many times over the summer that she knew some of the words by heart.

"Away down south by the Southern Sea, an elephant sits in a cinnamon tree."

Charlotte turned the pages to the monkey, the kitten, Granny Faddle, the fair, Wicked Willie … and there was the little girl on Clatter Street wearing a red coat and bonnet, which Charlotte thought were pretty. She turned the bedcovers back down and turned off the flashlight. The house was dark but for her nightlight.

Charlotte got out of bed, set the book back in her doll trunk, and tiptoed to her mother's door, which was partly ajar. She pushed it open a little bit more. Charlotte listened to the room. She couldn't hear her mother. With her flashlight in hand, she walked closer.

Jessie's bed was on the left wall, filling nearly a third of the room just inside the door. She and Matthew had liked the new, fashionable blond furniture, and their bed had a bookshelf headboard. Charlotte stood there, looking at her mother's closed eyes. She leaned down close to her mother's face and gently lifted one eyelid with her index finger to expose an eye.

Jessie smiled at her little girl, lifted the corner of the covers, and moved over to make room. Charlotte crawled into bed and settled her head, placing her nose close to her mother's face. When Jessie fell back asleep, Charlotte stayed close, feeling the breath from her mother's nose—in and out, in and out—assuring her that it would not stop. Then she too fell asleep.

CHAPTER 2

All was quiet in the little burg the next morning, Sunday morning. There would be no laundry machines or vacuum sweepers running. The day was reserved for churchgoing, and that was where Jessie began her Sunday mornings too.

Charlotte and Charles followed closely behind Jessie as she entered the small sanctuary of their new church in West Emmette. It was not a new church to Jessie, since she had grown up here, and it did feel good to her to return to the white, steepled structure built in 1901 next to the Civil War cemetery. Jessie walked to the left aisle side and counted five pews up of eight, entered the pew row, and chose their seats. The darkened, worn oak benches creaked as each member arrived and sat down in place.

Esther, the organist, was playing a prelude arrangement of "The First Noel," and Jessie quietly hummed along. She carried a black patent leather purse with a solid arched handle. In it were her husband's handkerchief, some SenSen breath fresheners, her tan wallet, and a pencil. They had unpacked their church clothes and shoes yesterday, and Jessie had found two one-dollar bills to place in the offertory plate. Jessie wore her white cotton gloves, and so did Charlotte.

The Reverend Edison Burchard began the service by welcoming the Conrads; then he asked for prayers for two members who were ill. Now he began reading his composed prayer, based on the New Testament scripture he would soon explain.

Jessie's thoughts wandered. *Do not be too hasty in your plans*, she recalled—words her Columbus minister had written to her five days after the accident. In that October letter, he then offered the name of a lawyer, a member of the church, writing, "He would be most happy, I am sure, to assist you in any way possible." And: "I am sorry I could not remain for the meal after the service." His penmanship and the blue ink were so ... bold, she recalled.

Jessie opened her eyes to this sanctuary, thinking of her mildly nearsighted vision. She took in the whole picture before her—a slightly blurred gathering of people she knew; the splashes of green, blue, red, and white decorations; the rows of pews and scrolled rails; the family sitting in front of her. She tried to see it all together. She wasn't listening to the minister completely, instead thinking about the miracle of her faith and the story of Jesus's birth. *So wondrous*, she thought.

How can it be? It gets so lost in the ribbon of church. Who is that sitting in the choir? she wondered, not recognizing one of the faces. She felt comfortable in her place, back in the pews here. She sat, relaxed, and wondered why. Then suddenly she craved eggnog and wondered whether the town store had any for purchase yet. *Maybe Dad and Ada have some*, she thought.

After church and after many members had hugged them in loving welcome, Jessie and Charlotte still had their white church gloves on as they, with Charles, drove back down Main Street to Jessie's childhood home, where her father stepped outside to greet them.

"Welcome home, my child," he said to his daughter, holding her tightly in his arms. "And here are my two favorite grandchildren," Henry Marshall Hall said to Charles and Charlotte, letting go of Jessie and whisking Charlotte up to his boxy, thick wool coat. He gave her a big kiss on the cheek. "Remember me?" he asked joyfully. Then he looked at Charles. "Hey, young man." He freed his right arm to extend a handshake. "How are you, Charles?"

"Fine, sir," Charles replied.

"The country has a new president, Charles. What do you think of Mr. Kennedy?"

"Well, we'll see," Charles replied as his mother would have said. His grandfather chuckled in agreement.

As they walked toward the back door of the house, Henry said to his daughter, "I have Matthew's funeral book for you. Frank at the funeral home finished it and left it with me for you."

"Yes." Jessie knew. "Good."

"I noticed a few names of guests I missed seeing."

They stepped inside. After he helped Charlotte remove her coat, Henry reached for the book on his desk. "The only flowers the funeral parlor staff couldn't find cards for were some white ones—artificial, I think—in a small vase or jar of some sort and a basket of plants with some violets in it," Henry said.

"The large plant basket was from Matthew's trucking company," Jessie said.

"Oh." Henry nodded. "Ada has kept that basket for you. You can take it home today. And we have that little vase too. And two others."

"I'll give one to Ada," Jessie said.

"Do you recall that the colonel came to calling hours?" he said.

Just then Ada, Henry's sister, walked into the room. "Hi, kids," she said, looking at Charles and Charlotte. "Are you going to school tomorrow?"

❄ ❄ ❄

"Can't we just forget about school till after Christmas?" Charlotte said in the car during their return home. Jessie drove past the brick school building and Schiller's Garage, then turned onto Meadow Drive, knowing they would indeed have to face a new school—and tomorrow too.

That evening after tucking Charles and Charlotte into bed, Jessie sat at her desk and opened the funeral book. There were Emma and Warner's names. The funeral home room floated back to her. She looked down into the pages of lines; there among the signatures were the scrolled names of her bakery coworkers and of Matthew's truck driver buddies … So many friends. That evening had been so muffled.

In the darkness outside, flurries of snow began to drop through the chilled night air. Jessie pulled open her desk drawer and lifted out an envelope from Matthew's mother, who had stayed with her during the first few days after the accident. When Matthew's mother had returned home, she mailed this poem to her daughter-in-law, which a friend had sent to her, having heard it on the Gary Moore radio show. Jessie reread it now. It was titled "God's Lent Child."

> I will lend you, for a little time,
> A child of mine, He said,
> For you to love the while he lives,
> And mourn for when he's dead.

It may be six or seven years,
Or twenty-two or three,
But will you, till I call him back,
Take care of him for Me?

Jessie read on to the end of the poem, then folded the thin paper on which dear Mabel had typed it, and placed it in the back of the funeral book. She turned the small, cold knob on the metal, gray desk lamp beside the twine-wrapped desktop wishing well Matthew had made for her and wept.

CHAPTER 3

The 1900 single-story, rust-red brick school building sat snugly on a slightly risen embankment off Main Street. It required three steps up from the slate sidewalk and twenty paces to the plain twin front doors and large-pane front windows, nearly across from the Henry Hall home. The playground behind the school building joined a number of backyards on Meadow Drive below the hill. Jessie drove Charles and Charlotte to that building the next morning, December 5. Charlotte, wearing her white-collared church dress, black patent shoes of yesterday, and a gray coat and wool hat tied at the chin, clutched her purse for the ride. It held her stuffed dog, Spot.

Jessie nervously pulled into a visitor's parking space, lightly dusted with snow, near the front door. Her car seemed too big. A man walked outside from the front doors to greet them. He was tall and looked like that singer Jack Jones. His suit was brown.

"Hello, Jessie," he said warmly, taking her hand as she got out of the car. The brother and sister stepped slowly out of their back seats and into the bright, chilly December morning. "So this is Charles and Charlotte. How do you do?" He directed his attention to them.

He reached out to shake Charles's hand and then Charlotte's. "I am your principal. Come!" he said happily. "Come! Your teachers are anxious to meet you. Jessie, you can finish the paperwork in the office. We are just beginning classes. We can all walk in together."

Soon Charles was whisked away by a woman waiting inside the front door; she took him down a wide, dim, open hallway; and Mr. Powell walked Jessie and Charlotte to another wooden door nearby. He knocked, then opened the classroom door and guided Charlotte to the front of a large, bright classroom while Jessie watched.

He said to the teacher, "This is Charlotte."

The woman looked down at Charlotte with a warm, genuine smile, leaned over a little, and said to her, "I'm Mrs. Dolman, your new teacher. Welcome to our first grade." She bid goodbye to Mr. Powell and Jessie. Jessie bit back a few tears as Mrs. Dolman led Charlotte by the hand a few steps forward to the teacher's desk at the front of the color-tabbed room. The chalkboard behind them had Charlotte's name on it.

"Class," she sang out, "this is Charlotte Conrad. She will be joining our class today. She has moved here from Columbus, Ohio. Susan, will you show Charlotte to her seat?"

And right there, a life-long friendship began—not only with the girl Susan but also with school and Sebastian, a boy Charlotte didn't notice that day. Thirty years later he would tell her the color of the dress she wore on that Monday: green.

There were a few books and a tablet waiting for Charlotte on her desk. A first-grade workbook was on the top. It was yellow with a reddish color, and it had a picture of a boy and girl picking apples on the front. It was different from her book back in Columbus. This one looked … okay. Charlotte lifted the front cover.

"Class, let's turn to page thirty-eight in your reading book. Steve, would you read the first three lines on page thirty-eight?"

The boy stood up and read, "A big tree grew in a—" But he paused when he came to the word *meadow*.

Sebastian's eyes were still watching the new girl. Charlotte could not take her eyes off the new box of crayons, wishing to open them now.

❄ ❄ ❄

In the school office, Jessie was finishing the transfer papers. The records had arrived from Columbus. Charles had been an A student. "He will like Mrs. Irvine, Jessie," the secretary said. "She's one of our best teachers—in the entire school system. Sign one more line here," she said, pointing. She looked up at Jessie. "How are you doing? How is Charles doing? Is he adjusting all right?"

Jessie said, "He has been quiet. A little more quiet. But otherwise he seems okay. I think he is trying to step up and fill his dad's shoes already somehow." She looked down at the papers with a clenched smile.

The secretary placed her hand on Jessie's. "Mrs. Irvine is a kind and wise woman with a loving heart. She has been here for twenty years. She will be loving, and at the same time she will challenge Charles. She'll be of help." The mimeograph machine, with its clicking drum and perfuming ink, finally finished its printing assignment on the wall table across the room.

"Jessie, do you have a minute?" Principal Frank Powell had stepped out of his adjoining office. She followed him to his desk.

"You asked me whether there were any part-time jobs here at the school. As a matter of fact, Mr. Lions would like to retire at the end of the month as the school crossing guard at the street here in front of the building. It's a small job for now … but if you are interested, it requires an hour at the beginning of the school day and at the end. It pays two dollars per hour. You are welcome to the job if you want it."

"I've only ever worked in a bakery during the war before the children were born," Jessie replied. "But I would like the job. I'll need it. And of course that enables me to be near the children."

"The job is through the police department. Chief Briicker will come by with your hat and vest and go over things at your house before school resumes in January. You'll do fine, Jessie. I'm glad you're interested."

He walked Jessie back to the front office. "I think Charlotte and Charles will be happy here. We'll see to it. If you have any questions, just ask us, Jessie," he added, motioning to the secretary, then excused himself back to his desk.

The secretary continued, "Has Charles met any boys on his street yet?"

"Yes. Well, yesterday Charles met Jackie Walker. Our next-door neighbors are the Walker family."

"Oh," the secretary said flatly. "Jackie. Well … Charles will meet other boys today too. I think a few more live on Meadow. It's a growing street."

"You are but a child and always will be." Where had she heard that thought? Jessie wondered, repeating it now as she took another tray of cookies from the oven the following week. The house was in better order, and most belongings were unpacked and in place, including the kitchen supplies. They had even found and set up a Christmas tree this week, she and Charles. Even with the head of the family gone, the children were to get some presents and their Christmas cookies: while the children were in school, Jessie was baking their favorite first—soft gingerbread men. The recipe from her spiraled, heavily marked cookbook called for nearly two jars of molasses—the deep amber color of which surprised her every year—and brown sugar, eggs, sour milk, vanilla … lots of flour. This was a recipe she had learned while working at the bakery; she now tubed the decorator's frosting on the gingerbread bellies as buttons.

Christmas cards were arriving in her post office box—a welcome shift from sympathy cards and insurance mail, though these cards were addressed to Mrs. Jessie Conrad, not Mrs. Matthew Conrad. Jessie taped the holiday cards one by one to the birch attic closet door between the kitchen and living room. Their pictures were colorful and glittered and happy. The cards' art flapped outward with sleighs and Santas and wreaths and the word *Joy.*

Had it really happened? Was she really here? Alone? In West Emmette?

Jessie looked at her left hand and her wedding band. *Just because he's dead doesn't mean he's … dead,* Jessie thought. She placed the last of the cookie men into a storage box and took them to the cold garage to store them on the shelves. Her hands were heavy, slow. She added the years in her mind again … 1944 … 1960. They had been married sixteen years.

The sky and light outside dulled to a gray, and with it there began to fall a rain of snow, then quickly a heavier snowfall onto the newly adopted ground. There were no cardinals within sight of the window to enjoy, since there were no trees in the yard yet for perch. The cardinals were next door, over at the Walker's. There were no train whistles in the distance here. No tulip or daffodil bulbs in the earth yet. No rose bushes in wait.

It was so very good of Bill to let them move in. *The check from Columbus should be coming soon,* she thought. *And the insurance check.* Jessie was listening to a recording of the song "Sleigh Ride" on the hi-fi. The cheerful prance of tune and happy heartbeat of bells lifted her spirits. Jessie placed the plastic electric window candle, a tier of eight red Christmas bulbs, in the front living room window and plugged it in. Its glow was an immediate promise, a steady friendship. Maybe she would be able to sleep better tonight. In her blue house slippers, she carried the two smaller candle tiers of three red bulbs each to Charlotte's bedroom window and then to her own, completing the street front decorations. And declaration.

Jessie returned to the kitchen table. It was soon time to pick Charlotte and Charles up from school. She and Charles would need to shovel the driveway. She opened a card from the Wolfes, their neighbors and dear friends in Columbus. She sat at the table in silence. Emma wrote to ask whether they could come for a visit. It might help Walter, who was having some trouble adjusting to Charles's move. Jessie thought of young Walter, how he and Charles had done everything together as neighbors. They had been at school together, in Scouts together, and at church and camp together.

Charles hasn't mentioned Walter recently, Jessie thought. *Maybe it would be better to not see them again yet.* Jessie wrote an excuse to Emma in her reply but later thought she should ask Charles to write his own card to Walter. This was, as it would be, an important afterthought, as afterthoughts often are.

After bringing the children home from school, Jessie shared Emma's card with Charles and asked whether he would be willing to write a letter to Walter.

"What about my spelling?" he asked his mother.

"Don't worry about spelling this time," Jessie said, handing a sheet of paper to him along with a pencil. "You write good messages to me. Give it a try. It will mean a lot to Walter."

Charles took the task to his room, where his ball glove and baseball card collection sat atop his dresser. Charles sat on the floor, placed the large *Boys Life* magazine on his knees to brace the writing paper, and wondered what to say. He began.

> Hi Walter. We are ok. Our new house is on a
> street called Meadow Drive. We are across the
> street from a farm. I have my own room. It faces
> the backyard, which isn't planted yet. We have
> some snow. My new teachers name is Mrs. Irvine.
> She seems nice and the school seems ok. Mom got
> a job as the school crossing gard. She begins that
> in January. The school is smaller than ours was
> thare. What are you studying now?

Charles paused. "This is strange to write to Walter," he whispered aloud to himself. He wished they could play checkers together. He decided not to tell Walter about his new neighbor, Jackie. Besides, Jackie wasn't like Walter. Walter was more like a brother. In thought Charles tapped his pencil against his knee, then continued.

> Charlotte and I promise to stay your freind. Have
> a good Christmas. Charles.
> P.S. I helped Mom put up our tree.

While Charles's letter traveled to Walter's house, the holiday lights went on and off and on and off, and soon December 25 arrived. The three Conrads felt solemn in the task before them: to open presents without their husband and father. Jessie moved through the motions with her children with a cheerfulness that came from some reserve—a mysterious strength that came to her like a present left beneath the tree. Charles and Charlotte were able to move forward too—in the natural brightness of Christmas morning, in the inherent joy of the different day. They were to go to Grandma Conrad's house for dinner soon.

Charlotte lifted her new blue sweater out of the gift box from her mother and put the beautiful, soft sweater on after dusting her undershirt with the April Showers powder Santa had left for her; Charles also dressed in his new, long-sleeved, burgundy polo shirt. Before putting on her coat, Jessie placed around her neck the red crystal necklace Matthew had given to her last Christmas. The necklace had not one but two strands of red rhinestone beads, separated into sections by a golden inch of chain, and an occasional gold ball, similar in design to the great ceiling in the New York City Ballet Theatre, a place she would never see. The necklace reminded Jessie of … a cardinal.

Before December ended, the police chief Scott T. Briicker came to the front door of 147 with Jessie's crossing guard uniform. Charles and Charlotte shrank backward out of the front room as the man, who was as tall as their Christmas tree, stepped through the doorframe, bending down to allow for the additional eight-inch height of his gray felt, four-dent Stratton sheriff's hat. On the front of the hat, above the stiff wide brim, was a metal badge, and his jacket was clasped tightly with a belt and shouldered with a cross harness and another badge. The man was wearing a gun, and to the children it was as though Sky King himself had stepped into their home.

"Good evening, Jessie," he boomed. He caught sight of Charles and Charlotte, who ducked into the hallway. "I brought your gear."

"Hi, Scott. Come in. Thank you." She gazed at the objects in his arms. "How is Eleanor?"

"She's well. She's had a flare-up of bronchitis, but otherwise she's well." He began to hand a wooden stop sign on a handle to Jessie. "This is your stop sign, which I'll show you how to hold up in a minute. This is … You'll need to put this reflective harness across your coat each shift. And you'll need to wear this hat." He grinned, handing her a black eight-point police hat. "You are an official deputy now, you know."

He looked about the floor space, stepping a little more into the room. "Let me show you what you'll do." He pretended to step into a road, which would be Main Street. "When the road is clear of traffic, you step out into the street and hold up the sign— hold it out and up like this. You stand in the middle of the street, stopping any approaching cars for children to cross. You know. You walk with them to the other side and wait for the next child." He lowered the sign. "I'll meet you the first school morning in January, okay? It's easy. It requires common sense, is all. I know you have that in buckets."

After Scott bid her good night and returned to his patrol car, Charles tried on the deputy hat, and Charlotte ran out to the living room, wearing the play pistol and the cowgirl boots Grandma Conrad had given to her for Christmas. The cowgirl boots were really grand. Jessie let Charlotte blow the whistle Scott had also appointed to her; and quietly, after Jessie had closed the front door, Scott Briicker pulled a shovel from his car and cleared a little more snow from the Conrads' driveway by the street before leaving and driving down Meadow.

The world outside had turned blue under the midnight sky and did not seem at all natural. It was alive with the glitter of snow and did not seem like night. At two a.m. Jessie lifted her bedcovers to the side, swung her petite feet to the bedside rug, picked up her alarm clock, and set it down again, unable to sleep. The wind blew with a brisk howl outside the window, and she knew there was more snow with it. She stood and paced across the room … for what?

She looked around for something. She wouldn't want Christmas to end. That was it. What would the new year bring? How would she manage? "Dear God," she whispered, "I know You are here. Please help me to understand how to work with You. And how to hear You. And help me to come to know what the key is. It is such a beautiful world. Help me to protect my children, and help them to be happy and to find their way safely."

CHAPTER 4

I n the spring of 1961, for Charlotte's seventh birthday, Jessie
gave to her daughter a petal-pink jewelry box, a simple but
beautiful twelve-inch object of art with a gold-colored fluted
knob and a gold-embossed, lightly padded leatherette top. Jessie
followed Charlotte as she ceremoniously carried the amazing gift
to her room, where Charlotte looked about for the proper place
to set it, and she chose the old, newly painted bookcase.

Later, behind her closed door, in the quiet of evening,
Charlotte unlocked her doll trunk with the small silver key,
took her pink rhinestone ring from the doll shoe, and, lifting the
lovely lid of the jewelry box, placed the ring in the center slot
of the raised felt tier. She had already placed a necklace inside,
the one Charlies had given to her that morning. Her mom didn't
know about the ring or who had given it to her. It was her secret.
Charlotte closed the box lid gently and did a few Chaînés ballet
turns on the floor before it; then she raised her arms into fifth

position, in a perfect arch above her head in the way Mr. Sheldon had taught her back home.

By April's end, temperatures were warming, the landscape snow was melting, and construction on Meadow Drive resumed, with three more lots in development. On Saturday morning Charles hurriedly broomed the garage and patio and ran to the new lot being dug right across the street. Instead of finding his friend Bobbie Braunhall there, however, there stood Robert Zimmer, drawing something on a matchbook cover.

"Hey there, young man," he said to Charles, who came to a quick halt.

"Hey," Charles replied, out of breath.

Mr. Zimmer was still drawing. "So you're the fellow who bought 147."

"Yessir."

"How do you like it?"

"I like it a lot."

"I built it, you know."

Charles took that in and wondered about it, muttering a thank-you with his young frame of reference. "What are you doing?" he asked.

"Mapping out the next one." Mr. Zimmer was holding a matchbook cover open, and there were some squares sketched on the inside cover. They were standing, the two, at the edge of the dug-out foundation. "If you boys are playing over here when we aren't working, be careful, ya hear?"

"Yessir."

That wasn't the only lot Bob and Bill Zimmer and their brothers were working on. The men had added five streets in town already, and Meadow Drive was number six. Thistle Lane had just been completed, and the Zimmers' sister, Shirley, was now planting sycamore trees along its roadside.

Jessie stepped outside again and gazed at the exposed yard, still in its ungroomed, raw state. A bluebird flew to the new address and set himself atop the lamppost, watching Jessie. The cool, fresh air brushed Jessie's temple, where she measured the temperature. The wisps of her hair, just cut to the shorter length she had longed for for so long, and also lightly permed, brushed playfully at her cheek. This felt good. Was Matthew nearby? she wondered. He wouldn't have liked her haircut.

Jessie didn't feel as frightened as she had felt in October and December. Six months had passed now. Jessie was watching for the cars to arrive, and here they came, up the street, the two Conrad cars pulling into the straight, short driveway atop Meadow. Jessie greeted her husband's family once again. This time they were in their outdoor work clothes and had come to clear the yard.

Charles, now nine, was dressed to work too and ran back to his house across the street. Robert Zimmer glanced over with a smile as he saw Charles pull his father's shovel and wheelbarrow from the garage and wheel them to the front yard, which was now fully thawed and showing the construction lumps of the previous fall. Gordon arrived with two small trees—maple. Nelle brought a set of white plastic decorative yard ducks, a mother duck and two ducklings, which Jessie thought were so cute.

The three women, two men, Charles and Will, and now another cousin, Nelle's son, Andrew, set about digging up rocks and raking the ground. There were many lucky stones and pieces of limestone and sandstone—some large—and it was Charlotte's job to put them in buckets. She slipped one smooth and extra-white lucky stone into her pocket.

At the end of the afternoon, the family gathered on the patio for a rest and some lemonade. The women sat on Jessie's green glider; the men sat in lawn chairs, and Charles and Charlotte and Will and Andrew sat on the picnic table bench, all of which Jessie had wiped clean earlier in the morning. When Bill Zimmer had sold the house to Jessie, he had instructed his brother to install a simple awning to the back porch cement slab, something they usually left up to the new owner.

"Here we are again," Gordon said.

There were a few moments of silence as everyone's muscles slumped into rest. Gordon looked at his sister, Nelle, his eyes acknowledging the absence of Matthew.

Gordon continued, deciding to turn the loud silence into something jovial. "Remember when we used to sit on our front porch back home on the farm on Sundays while growing up?"

Nelle nodded, dropping her head in a smile. "Yeah. After church?"

"And after lunch," Gordon said. "Remember, we would go out to the porch. Mom would hardly be done gathering dishes, and we'd be sitting out there."

Nelle said, "And a car would pull in—"

"Toot the horn and pull up," Gordon added, "and out would jump—"

"Crazy Willie." Nelle's smile stretched.

Gordon continued, "And he'd join us on the porch, raise his nose—"

"And ask us if there were any leftovers." Nelle laughed.

"And before we could even tell Ma he was there, out she'd come with a plate," Gordon recalled.

"Then another car would pull in," Nelle added.

"Yep. And another." Gordon laughed. "And then came Howard," he said with playful sarcasm, lifting his hands in surrender, smiling at his brother-in-law. "And before we knew it, we had a porch full."

Jessie, swirling her lemonade in the gold-leafed glass, where the ice cubes sounded like small bells, glanced at Margaret, and recalled the letter Margaret's neighbor had sent to her the week after the funeral in October. The neighbor wrote to Jessie such casual small talk—it was so unnatural—saying that her husband had a sore throat and that she needed to take her mother to the doctor for some minor thing. She'd rambled on and on about nothing.

"How long would everyone stay?" Charles asked. "On the big, old front porch, I mean."

"All afternoon," his aunts and uncles said together.

"Sometimes till dark," Gordon said.

"If we got to singing," Nelle added.

They all were nodding, remembering.

"Singing what?" Charles asked.

"'Oh we ain't got a barrel of money,'" Nelle sang, beginning the melody.

"'Maybe we're rag-ged and funny,'" Gordon continued in song.

"'But we travel along,'" the group joined in, "'singin' our song, side by side.'"

"It's yours, Jessie!" Gordon prompted. She had the prettiest voice.

"'Through all kinds of trouble,'" she sang alone, "'what if the sky should fall.'"

She wanted to cry but didn't.

Nelle and Margaret joined her. "'Just as long as we're together.'"

Then everyone sang, "'It doesn't matter at all!'" Charlotte and Charles knew the lyrics, since they had performed the song for their father one night, and they sang along too, to the last verse. "'Just travelin' along, singin' our song, side … by … side.'" The group clapped and laughed.

❋ ❋ ❋

That night when the children were getting into bed, Charlotte tucked the lucky stone under her pillow, and Charles showed his mother something he had pulled from his pocket before she put his pants into the laundry hamper.

"I found this today in the yard."

"Oh!" Jessie said, taking the piece from his hand, her voice full of wonder. "This is an arrowhead. Where did you find it?"

"In the back, in the dirt, while raking."

"Tomorrow we'll take it to Grandpa Hall after church."

On Sunday noon, Charlotte marched up the wooden porch steps and into her grandfather's house behind her brother and mother. When Charles showed the deep-gray flint to his grandfather, Henry Hall told Charles and Charlotte to pull up a chair. They were in their grandpa's sitting room on the right side of the old house, where Henry's rifle collection was encased on the back wall.

Charlotte felt uneasy in this room. It was dim, crowded, and old. And now Grandpa Hall had also begun to collect and repair clocks in his retirement, and ten clocks of various sizes lined the walls. There was a constant soft drone of many light, high *tick-ticks* and slow, deep *clawk-clawks* marching time through her veins and head and—

"Here's the story," their grandfather began. Henry sat down across from the children on his mill stool, and he scooted it a bit closer to them. He was a small man with a talent and wisdom beyond his hometown. Years before, he had inherited the grain and flour mill across the street and ran it well, and while doing so, he had written a reference book about the Kentucky rifle, his passion. During World War II, at the request of the government, Henry closed his mill at age fifty-eight to be the region's army ordnance weapons inspector. After the war, he sold the mill property to the Zimmers, who converted the lot into their lumber mill and building center.

He began, "Our state of Ohio is known as 'the mound builders state.'"

"What's that?" Charlotte asked.

"They were made by Indians," Charles said.

"No, well, not exactly," their grandfather said. "When white men first came to Ohio land, they found these peculiar large mounds of earth and stone. When they asked the American Indians if they had made them, the Indians said they did not, that the mounds had been there when they first came here to Ohio. Anyway, the very ancient people who built the mounds came to be called, by archeologists and historians, the 'Mound Builders.'"

"Where did they come from?" Charles asked.

"How they reached our continent can only be guessed. Many believe the people came from Asia, reaching America by the Bering Straits."

Charles looked at his flint. "When?" he asked.

"Maybe three thousand years Before Christ." Henry went on. "The Mound Builders' pottery and weapons"—he glanced at Charlotte, who was looking at the intricately carved brass stem bell on her grandfather's desk top—"and jewelry have been found in these mounds of theirs.

"The oldest group of these people of aborigines are called by scientists the 'Fort Ancient' people. They were the most numerous. There is another later group called the 'Hopewell Culture.' Their weapons and pottery were shown to be more advanced, with excellent workmanship.

"Southern Ohio contains the most mounds in North America. More than five thousand!" He looked at Charlotte. "But guess what? I located one right here in our township. Have you seen the hill going up Spade Road, on the right side there as you go to the dump? That big hill? To the right from there, there is a raised mound that covers about fifty feet by one hundred feet covered by stone and forest trees. Some of our earliest settlers refer to its terraced opening by the spring as the 'Indian Hole.'"

Charles's eyes widened. "I'll take you up there soon," Henry said. "Here is a piece I found up there." He took a cloth bag from his desk drawer and withdrew a curious object. "I showed this to the Ohio state people, the historical society group, and they logged it in their Atlas." Charles and Charlotte looked at the item, a sort of horn made of bone. Henry paused to take another draw on his pipe. His lips made a small popping sound around the mouthpiece.

"What happened to those people?" Charles asked.

"They became extinct, amazingly." Henry squinted in thought and wonder anew. "Now let me look at your flint," Henry said to Charles, drawing again on his pipe with some excitement. Charles handed the flint to his grandfather, and Henry looked closely at it. He turned the pointed end of the notched flat stone in his hand. "The chipping of flint is quite a process, Charles. To begin, a man would select a chippable stone or material like obsidian flake or flint or a mineral like chert or quartz and strike it with a stone hammer or even another stone and then use a bone or antler and chip off the corners to shape it for whatever purpose he needed."

"What was this doing in our yard?" Charles said. Charlotte so wanted to ring the bell.

"Well," Henry said. "When the Zimmers blasted or excavated that ground up there for homes, they culled up some long-buried things, I guess. Treasures." Henry thought the word *treasures* would catch Charlotte's fancy. He glanced at her and said, "If you would like to ring that bell, sweetheart, go ahead."

Charlotte picked up the three-inch, delicate bell by its four-inch-long stem handle, and with barely a movement of her small hand, the bell rang a loud, beautiful tone. "Most bells are made of a mixture of copper and tin, Charlotte, but that one is made of fine brass. It was my mother's."

Charlotte, satisfied, set the slender piece carefully back on the desktop. Henry continued. "Even if Meadow Drive was once farmland, before your street was cut in, the farmer would not have tilled up the earth as deeply for planting crops as builders do for basements. Thus, construction digging turns up some long-buried items sometimes. Anyway, your flint is probably Indian. It's beautiful."

Charlotte asked timidly to be excused and rose from her seat to find her mother. She walked past the pioneer rifles and the wall where there were certificates, documents, and some framed photos of her grandfather standing with some military men. Grandpa was in a suit in the pictures. The military men in the photos had medals on their uniforms. Some other wall hangings were framed newspaper and magazine articles about Grandpa.

Charlotte found her mother in the kitchen with Aunt Ada. Charlotte didn't like Grandpa's sister, Ada, very much. Her kitchen smelled strange. Ada was at some machine, putting carrots and celery into it. And was that spinach?

"Charlotte!" she said. "Go out to the coop and get me an egg." Ada looked dryly at the girl. "No, get two."

Charlotte was glad to go outside. This was the house where her mother had grown up, and the old chicken coop was still in use. The chickens were wandering about the dirt driveway. Charlotte walked out into the backyard toward a garden patch, which was freshly tilled for planting.

Just then Uncle Bird pulled into the driveway in his old pickup truck, scattering the strolling chickens into a fast trot. He saw Charlotte at the garden and strode with his long legs through the lumped, high grass over to her and picked her up. He smelled like paint. Bird was a tall, lanky man, and being lifted so high scared Charlotte; she grabbed hold of his suspender.

"What are you looking for, sweet pea?" he asked. The man's expression was always rather blank behind his big eyeglass frames, and it was never clear on his long, bony face whether he was smiling.

Suddenly Charlotte heard a strange rumble, and Bird, still holding Charlotte high in his arms, turned his big glasses to the left, looking toward Main Street. Charlotte looked to the right across the yard, then to the ground far below. She thought the sound, growing louder, was in the ground. The volume expanded and seemed closer. Bird also looked to the ground and worried about an earthquake. Charlotte turned her eyes to the sky and saw a large, dark cloud approaching. She pointed at it, and Bird saw the cloud too. It was reflected in his glasses as it got closer, and the two stood completely still in astonishment.

The loud rumble and fast-moving, stretching cloud was a swarm of bees! A large swarm of thousands of bees moving in direct sail together—moving right over the tall man and little girl, who were silent at the sight but unafraid—was flying toward the large ash tree in the backyard, and the buzzing flock began to enter a hole in the tree at an upper split in the trunk, where the tree trunk formed a Y into two upper arches of budding canopy.

They watched until all the cloud slowly poured into the tree, and the great noise of their flight quieted. Charlotte turned her little face toward the glasses on the bony, white-topped head of her quiet relative, and the man gently loosened his guarded hold on Charlotte and carefully set her down. The two held hands, looking back up at the tree; then they thoughtfully stepped their big boots and little shoes across the ground to enter the house together and tell the others what they had witnessed.

That evening at the bathroom counter back home, while Jessie brushed Charlotte's hair—which was so soft from their well water—Charlotte said to her mom, "Who is Uncle Bird?"

"He's Grandpa's sister's husband," Charles said in all his big-brother tone, entering the bathroom and buttoning up his pajamas, which were getting to be a bit snug.

Jessie, lifting a section of Charlotte's hair to set a sponge curler, said with fondness, "You might remember my telling you that my mother died when I was one year old. Daddy raised us— your Aunt Ethel and me—alone for a long time, with the help of a woman down the street, Mae. Then one day years later, when Ethel and I were eleven and twelve, Grandpa's sister Ada's husband died, so Ada moved in with Daddy—her brother—to help with us girls." Jessie added a second curler. "Then just a few years ago, Ada married again. She married a good family friend, Bird."

Charlotte listened hard. "Why is his name Bird?"

"He's part Indian," Charles said, pulling open the second drawer, his drawer.

"Yes. He's a good man," Jessie said, her thoughts drifting. "You know," she added with soft regard, "Bird served in the war—World War I—and he was highly regarded by his officers. They wrote a beautiful letter about him to his mother when he was discharged in 1918. He was injured. Ada has the letter."

"Why is he so tall?" Charlotte asked.

"Because he's a good man," Jessie replied. "I like to imagine that a person grows taller with every good act."

Charles thought about that. "But Grandpa's short."

"Oh yes, you're right," Jessie said, looking at her son. "You're right. Well, that idea doesn't stand, does it?" She grabbed her son in a tickle tackle and chased him into his room. She tickled his sides through his thick pajamas, and Charles laughed then ran to chase his sister, who had followed them to the doorway. Charlotte darted into her room and began to hurriedly close her door, but Charles pushed it open. The three laughed during the fun chase until Charles got too rough and Charlotte screamed, "Stop! Stop!"

Jessie said, "All right, that's enough," and she drew her hand over Charlotte's quilt to smooth it out. The floral patch quilt was always cool to the touch; it had been made by her dear Aunt Mae, as they called her, from the fabrics of her old housedresses. "What book shall we read tonight?"

"The book Aunt Nelle brought yesterday!" Charles called.

Charlotte hopped down and went over to the book box her father had made for them and drew out *The Little Train That Saved the Day*, the book whose author was also named Charlotte.

"No!" Charles yelled. "The new one!" And he ran across the hall to get the book his aunt had brought.

"No! I want my book!" Charlotte argued. Nelle had brought one for Charlotte too. The book cover illustration of light blues and greens had a little girl pictured at the seashore, and Charlotte exchanged the old yellow and black cover for the new book.

"Okay," Jessie said, "We'll read Charles's first." Charles jumped back up on the bed next to Charlotte. "Charles, how about you read it to us."

Jessie, Charlotte, and Charlotte's stuffed animals listened to Charles read clearly and easily. Charlotte held her own book and half listened. Charles looked over at Charlotte. "If you hold your book up too straight, all the commas and periods are gonna slide right straight off the pages and into your lap!"

Before going to sleep that night, Charlotte hid her brother's new copy of *Boys' Life* magazine in her bottom dresser drawer under the paper liner below the spare blanket.

In his room before going to sleep, Charles sorted and counted his round glass marbles with their glass mystery. *Thwack!* He placed a few on the floor and practiced shooting. *Thwack! Thwack!* He aimed the shooter at the blue beauty. He then added a new Indian nickel to his collector's book and crawled into bed.

In her room, Jesse reread the letter from Pigeon Bodie, which had been forwarded from Columbus to the new West Emmette address and delivered only yesterday. It invited the three of them to move in with their family in their new home in Cleveland, if need be. Pigeon's husband, Chase, had driven a truck with Matthew for eight years, but last year he had been transferred to the Cleveland depot. Jessie continued reading.

Pigeon wrote that Chase's mother had also heard the news of Matthew's accident on the radio, but she didn't send Pigeon and Chase the newspaper clipping until now. Pigeon was upset that no one had called them right away. Chase took the news "rather badly," saying Matt was his "buddy on the acid train … and a true friend."

Jessie thought of their picnics together. Both couples had waited to start a family for a few years after the war. "With help from the Almighty," she wrote to Jessie, "I know you'll come through this and be an even greater gal than you already are." Then she invited Jessie and Charles and Charlotte to come. "I know you need a rest. Why don't you pack the car and come to stay with us, just as long as you'd like? You could even put the children in school here."

Jessie marveled at Pigeon's generous invitation. Pigeon didn't know she and the children had left Columbus. Her words were full of love and concern, and Jessie's heart swelled at the sincerity and generosity in her friend's six-page-long letter. She would try to reply now, and she took up her pencil and stationery pad, and began the story of their new home in West Emmette. She would try to make ends meet here, she wrote to her friend.

CHAPTER 5

Jessie opened the kitchen window, reaching over the sink and sliding up the sash as spring swelled into summer. The outdoor thermometer, mounted outside on the window frame, read 68 degrees already. Around town girls and women were riding in cars and trucks with their hair tied up in ponytails and bandannas. Men and boys were back in T-shirts and farm hats, and transistor radios were in pockets and purses. The tart, green smell of ragweed waved up from the roadsides as cars with wide-open windows and bicycles passed by.

The churn of the Walkers' lawnmower next door came into the kitchen. Today's pie would be strawberry. Jessie pulled out the ingredients for the crust—the bag of flour, cooking oil, water, and salt. Charles and Charlotte were over at the Bauer farm, picking the berries. "They have no idea what's coming today," Jessie whispered to herself with a raised brow and nervous smile. She closed her eyes and inhaled slowly to steady the hour.

At ten a.m., just after the brother and sister set their berry buckets on the kitchen counter, having walked up the backyard from the farmland across Midville Road, a delivery truck backed into the Conrads' narrow driveway. Tommy, Bobby, Mitch, Cap, and Rooster were walking up the street with their ball gloves in hand to get Charles. Jessie's grass at 147 was coming up in its new, light-green growth, and the ground was solid enough for play. This yard was the longest and barest of all the upper Meadow Drive yards, since it bordered undeveloped lots on Midville Road and met the woods in the back. It was clear of trees and perfect for ball practice.

The mystery truck's tires came to a stop in front of the Conrad garage. Letters on the truck's side said "Kemple's Department Store," and the boys came running. Jessie stepped out of the house in her apron to meet the driver. Jackie ran over from next door to join the boys.

"Howdy, ma'am," the driver said. "Where do you want the piano?"

Charlotte watched through the front window.

"Right in the front door here," Jessie said, leading the man to the small porch. "Will it fit?"

"A piano?" the boys all yelled as Charlotte ran to the door and walked outside to her mother. Charlotte clasped her mom's hand tightly. What was happening?

The back of the boxy, white delivery truck was flung open, and two men clanked about, arranging straps and belts; and then it appeared, a large wooden instrument covered in cloth and bound by ropes. Slowly it was lowered with grunts and tugs, and the two men wheeled the piano on a cart to the front of the little house.

"How did this happen?" Ethel said to Jessie upon her visit the next day. Mondays were laundry days for both sisters, and

Tuesdays were ironing days. On Wednesday, Ethel had her hair done in the salon at Judy's house in town, then stopped at Jessie's afterward for lunch. Ethel's hair was prematurely white but thick, pretty, and still with curl. It was cut like most women's hair in town. This time Judy had puffed it up by ratting it a little too high and with extra hair spray. It wouldn't be moving in any weather.

Ethel was referring to the new spinet piano and standing in front of it with her sister and coffee cup. "It's beautiful, Jessie," Ethel said, sipping her coffee. "But ... well, *we* don't play the piano. What's the story?"

"Well," Jessie began, "you know the cemetery lots in Columbus that Matthew had bought for him and me. Of course, with Matthew's death being so unexpected, since we buried him here in the Conrad cemetery lot next to his dad, we don't need those lots in Columbus anymore, so I sold them."

"How?"

"I just called that cemetery office and explained, and they said a couple was looking for two spaces, and he gave me our money back."

"How much?"

"Seven hundred dollars. Exactly enough for this piano."

"But ... Jessie, you might need that money. What on earth made you want to buy a piano?"

"I want the kids to learn an instrument. Well, and you know I had to put away Charlotte's ballet things. I won't be able to afford dance lessons and costumes here." Jessie paused. "I heard piano is a good thing for children to know."

"Who told you that?"

"Well, I read it in the paper, and ... Daddy said so too, you know."

Ethel grinned. "Of course, Daddy." She thought of the nights she and Jessie had watched their father jam in their living room at home with his friends—their dad on sax, Frank on piano, Emmette on bass. "Who will teach them?"

"Mary Bauer."

❊ ❊ ❊

Bauer farm was a large section on the map, boxed across three hundred acres and forming a beach of patch-worked earth in view from the top of Meadow Drive. There was a stop sign at the top of Meadow, almost in symbolic message to the Zimmers, and beyond the intersecting ribbon of Midville Road was the farm. Henry Hall knew Donald Bauer well. When Henry had run the grist mill years before, Donald's father had brought his grain to the mill.

The Bauer family farmhouse, now in its third generation, was down Bauer Lane, which cut between the acreage a little below the top of Meadow on the other side. Mary's father, Arnold Leigh, lived in another farmhouse at the top and front, right across from the stop sign, with the orchard. The land beyond this two-story house, framed in green and white and with a grand front porch, rolled and dipped into gentle slopes, making it easy to see the fields, yet the rolls were gentle enough for tractors to easily navigate. A few miles east of the farm, the land began to drop much more dramatically into the deeply hilled terrain of Pennsylvania. No, this Bauer farmland was perfect Ohio land, with a nearly ideal climate—as ideal as a climate can be in northeast Ohio, even northeast America. All four seasons were reached in ultimate peaks.

Jessie loved it here. She was home. The ground felt and smelled comfortable under her feet, and it would help her heal.

In addition to her farm-wife duties, which were many, Mary Bauer also taught piano. When Jessie had bought some rhubarb at the farm earlier in the month, she asked Mary whether she was still giving lessons. Mary said she had a few students; Jessie told her she had ordered a piano.

"Well, yes I teach, Jessie, but remember, I only teach children to the intermediate level," she said. "I still do take on beginner students though. Summer's a great time to start. When does the piano arrive?"

"It's here," Jessie said proudly when she returned to the farm for more rhubarb the next week.

And so Mary soon followed the arrival of the piano. On Saturday, June 17, at ten o'clock, Mrs. Bauer came to the Conrad front door. She brought a brand-new piano book. Jessie let her in.

Mary greeted Jessie and looked at Charles and Charlotte. Charlotte's hair was tied into a ponytail with a pink ribbon. "Who's first?" Mrs. Bauer called out. Her voice was a pitch below Jessie's and double in volume. "Well, you know what? I think all three of us can fit on that piano bench. How about we get started together? Would that be okay? And then in another week, we'll take turns."

Jessie nodded with approval and moved to the couch. Charlotte sat down carefully on the bench to the right of Mrs. Bauer, and Charles shyly sat down on the left side—as far left as he could without falling off. Mrs. Bauer moved a coloring book from the piano's music stand and set the music book in its place. The new booklet had a drawing of a grand piano on the front, and the cover was printed in a reddish-orange color.

"This is book one of John Schaum's piano course," Mrs. Bauer began. She said this with serious regard; it was an introduction she had stated many times to many children, each time in its own magic and glory.

Mrs. Bauer, pausing to take in the shiny, new keys and piano frame, said, "This is a nice piano your mom bought. Cable Nelson," she read above the C key. "This piano name here, Cable Nelson, or any piano name is always placed above the center keys here." She pointed. "And this C is the center of the keys. There are eighty-eight of them. Have you both had a little music in school?"

"Yes, I did," answered Charles. "I know there are seven notes, A to G."

"I know just a little," Charlotte said timidly.

"Well, let's start at the beginning," Mrs. Bauer said. "Even if this is a review for you, Charles, you can just listen or help me." She pointed out the structure of an octave, and she played a simple scale. Her hands were the hands of a farmer's wife, tan and thick, with rough skin, her nails short for sorting beans and onions. Her piano lessons were on the simple and happy side, as was her own playing; she taught students for a little extra income, enough for the offering plate at their church.

"Just a dollar, Jessie, and a dollar for the book," she said while gathering her purse after the lesson. "Charles and Charlotte learned enough today to start practicing a first song." She looked about. "Do you have a tablet or something I could mark their lessons in?"

Charlotte and Charles had already run outside. Jessie went to the telephone stand and reached for her personal phone notebook. "Here," she said to Mary. "You can write in the back of this until I get a notebook for you to use."

Mary wrote down "The Wood-Chuck," the first song, and the beginning C-major scale. "I'll be back next Saturday." Mary paused. "Jessie, I don't know if you are interested, but our cat just had kittens. If you think Charlotte would like a kitten, they'll be ready in six or seven weeks. Free, of course." She laughed. Mary's laugh was the purest form of joy and confidence, bold and connected to the clouds.

Mary left, and Jessie lingered at the piano, looking at it with wonder, noticing the sweet smell of wood and ivory. She hummed the song "Money, Marbles and Chalk" on her way back to the kitchen. She was making bologna sandwiches for five. She and Charles were going to start painting the house light green. Her dad and Bird were bringing the ladders and paint.

❄ ❄ ❄

The temperature outside climbed to eighty-four degrees, and already it was a humid June afternoon. Jessie had a few shirts and pillowcases clipped to the clothesline—a metal pole with an umbrella-like clothesline anchored to the ground a few yards off the back patio. Gordon had installed the contraption. Charlotte used the other half of the plastic lines to create a tent, using the old bedspread her mom had draped there for that purpose.

Jessie was anchoring the corners of the bedspread with stones when Bird and her dad arrived, and then they quickly moved into the chore of painting. Bird took Charles to the left corner of the house with a can of paint and his own brush.

"Now you dip just the top half of the brush into the can," Bird instructed Charles. The boy did so. "That's right. Get a little bit more paint on the brush. Good. Now tap it inside the can a little to drop excess. That's it. Now make three blotches like this." Bird pushed three thick dabs of paint onto a small section of wood siding. "Now you brush it across the wood here ... drag your brush back and forth once ... that's it. Now dip again."

"Why do you put so much on?"

"Because the *Painters Magazine* says so," Bird answered with a knowing smile. "It's called 'flowing on' rather than 'brushing out.' You put a heavy dab out first, or two, and you drag it out and don't recross it more than necessary. That gives your wood a solid finish."

An hour passed as the four painted. Growing warm under cover, Charlotte stepped out of her tent, leaving her scrapbook behind, to find her weed bucket nearby and headed down the backyard. She stooped here and there, often pausing in distraction.

"What's Charlotte doing?" Henry said to Jessie.

"Digging dandelions. I pay her a quarter a bucket."

Henry watched Charlotte wander slowly from yellow cap to yellow cap with a blunt short tool and small plastic pail. "What's that she's singing?"

Jessie listened as her daughter's little voice carried over to her across the warm breeze. "'Green Door,'" she told her dad.

"Hmm." He chuckled, listening. Then to Jessie he said, "How is your ... how are you finding your monthly expenses, Jessie?"

"Well, you know," Jessie began, "selling the house so quickly in Columbus—thanks to Clyde next door—helped pay for this one. And it certainly helped and was generous of the Zimmers to let us move in before that check came in," she said. "Did you know, Dad, that Raymond and Kate offered to let us stay in the other side of their duplex if we didn't get a house right away?"

"Yes." Her dad nodded, gently dipping his brush again. *Good people*, he thought.

"And Pigeon and Richard invited us to stay with them even," Jessie added.

"I didn't know that," Henry said.

Jessie snapped her work smock shirt and reached for a tissue, coughing a little. Three crows landed in the backyard as clouds moved in front of the sun, casting a deep shadow and dimming the heat and bright light for a moment. "As you know," she continued, "there was the life insurance policy. Fifteen thousand dollars, which I've put away. And the Lutheran Brotherhood, two thousand. And our Social Security checks began in January. We get two hundred fifty-four dollars a month for the three of us."

"Did you get a lump sum death payment?"

"Yes. That was two hundred fifty-five. That came along in the first check."

The crows jumped in arches farther across the lawn as Charlotte moved closer to the tree line at the back of the yard. "I get four dollars a day for the school crossing guard job. I can pay the bills for now. I'll need to do something more next year though."

"Okay, well, you know to let me know when you need help," Henry added. He didn't have much in the bank, he knew. And Jessie knew. His savings were all in his collections.

"Sunsets are the worst part of the day for me," Jessie added quietly.

"Maybe light a candle in the evening," Henry suggested.

Bird was racing Charles's brush along on the wood, nearing the finish of applying their paint across the first six lower panels on the house's north side.

Henry continued in conversation with his daughter. "So Emmette found you a car."

"Yeah, Dad, the Pontiac made me feel sad ... and I need something smaller anyway. You know, I'm not real comfortable driving, especially any distance. The Corvair will get us around town." She brushed her dip of paint across a panel. "I saw an ad about Corvairs in Charles's scouting magazine. And Emmette said it is the new thing."

Emmette Schiller's garage and filling station was essentially the front porch of West Emmette. The garage lot was located on Main Street at the beginning of town and across from Burt's barbershop and the pharmacy. Paul Coyne had opened the pharmacy in 1959, just two years ago. The Zimmers had built one commercial building in town, a one-story structure that held the new pharmacy, the barbershop, and, to the rear of the pharmacy, an ice cream counter. A grocery store, housed in painted block, anchored the other end of town.

Schiller's Garage had formerly been a gas station with four fancy pumps and a staff of four in the 1930s. Now, reduced in mission, it was a repair garage with a workshop and a few used cars. Emmette III was a skeleton-thin man with white hair, bent slightly forward; he wore overalls that were shadowed with grease every day, every hour, except for funerals. He had been born old. No one knew his age, but everyone knew his family tree, and it was a great big, old tree.

Last week Jessie had pulled her husband's beloved 1952 Pontiac into Emmette's lot, and Emmette gave her the key to a 1960 Corvair. It was nearly an even trade, Emmette called it, though Henry quietly backed it after selling one of his rifles. When Jessie sat in the new Corvair's driver seat, so low to the ground, the compactness felt good. This was definitely more to her size and comfort.

"Now remember, Jessie," Emmette had said. "The engine is in the back. The trunk is in the front. Chevy says the rear engine improves the ride, traction, and breaking balance." He gently set his bony hand on the car roof. "It got 'Car of the Year' last year by *Motor Trend*." He was glad for that. "You'll get much better gas mileage, of course. Tank's filled up. I filled it earlier. Just take it home, Jessie. Take yer time. See how you like it."

Jessie was holding the steering wheel tightly, looking over the dash.

"Just take yer time. Drive up Meadow and around town a bit. Come and see me … you know, if you have any questions."

That day Jessie had looked left and right down Main Street to no traffic, then pulled slowly out of Emmette's lot. Without looking back at the Pontiac, she turned right to drive along Main Street through town along the elm trees past her old home, where her dad was on the front porch with one of his guns. Past the Lutheran church, she turned right up Midville Road, driving beside the fields of the Bauer farm on her left to the top entrance of Meadow Drive, then pulled the little, beige-colored Corvair into its new nest, the garage. It was a better fit, leaving room for the ladder and bicycles, a space Jessie and Bird went to now to get another ladder.

As the house painting continued, Bird and Charles moved to the back left side of the house, which was now in the shade, as the panels continued to change from whitewash to a soft hue of green.

"What made you choose light green for the house, Jessie?" Henry asked his daughter. "I like white, you know."

"I don't know, Dad. Of the many times we moved, we never lived in a green house. I just like it, I guess." Jessie and her dad were painting panels on the front of the house near the picture window and garage door. "The Leigh house is green up there," Jessie added.

Henry dabbed paint under the window frame, pulling the brush along carefully under the ridge. "How is the Wolfe family? And Charles's friend?"

"Walter?" Jessie said.

"Yes." Henry nodded.

"I received another letter from Emma," Jessie told him. "And you know we talk by phone." Henry knew Jessie and Matthew's neighbors in Columbus from visits there. "Emma said Walter is doing better, but he's still adjusting. Charles still doesn't know that Walter ran away when we moved."

"Walter really took it that hard, huh, when you moved away?"

Jessie nodded in concern. "He got two miles—almost two miles—into the nighttime, and the police found him at the railroad tracks near Camdon, on his wandering way to the station." Jessie's dry mouth clenched with regret. "They said Walter was cold and crying. Oh, Daddy, imagine. Imagine. He could have been hurt. Thank goodness the police spotted him."

Her face grew tense with the thought. "I hope they will come here and visit, maybe soon. It will never be the same, though." She looked into her father's eyes. "How do you explain that to a nine-year-old?" She paused. "Emma and I aren't sure what's best for the boys. Whether to come here. I guess it would be good to visit."

"I read recently that it's important to talk to young children about memories, Jessie," Henry said. "I read that you should spark conversations about events...or people. Like, you might want to ask Charles about Walter now and then, or recall an activity." Henry looked at his daughter, seeing her as a child in overalls among their chickens long ago. "You will want to do that about Matthew too," he said gently.

Jessie nodded, listening.

Henry wiped his brow with his handkerchief. "Clarence told me that Doris Ingalls is changing jobs at the paper."

"She writes the local township news for the *Post*, right?" Jessie said.

"Yeah. School board meetings, council meetings—that type of thing. She did that article about me once."

"That was really nice. It's pretty wonderful that your book is going into a second printing."

"You make sure you and Ethel keep at least four of those rifles. The ones featured in the book are in the case on the left wall. You know." He wiped a smudge of paint from the window glass, then tucked the rag back in his belt. "Ada wants me to sell them off, for her doctor bills. And, well, you know, I've given some of the guns to friends in the government, and," he added with hesitation, "I did lose one in a silly bet last October. The World Series," Henry said in a hushed voice. "I love the Pirates, you know. But who knew they would win."

Jessie resumed painting and dabbed paint into the corner panels near the garage. Charlotte, having finished a cherry Popsicle, was back under the blanket tent and falling asleep.

"So what do you think?" Henry said.

"About what?"

"Would you be interested in taking Ingalls's part-time job for the paper? It only involves ... well, maybe ten hours a week if that. When there's a meeting."

"I don't know the first thing about writing news, Dad."

"Well, would you want to talk to McClelland? He'll fill you in."

"Okay. I guess." The suggestion overwhelmed her, and she wondered how much she could do alone.

"First piano lesson was today," Jessie told her dad.

Henry smiled, pleased. "Did you hear about Kennedy's trip to Vienna?"

Henry moved on in conversation; and while the five family members at 147 continued in peaceful progress, Luther Walker swept sawdust, bent nails, and staples across the newest living room floor with his heavy bristled broom on Bloom Street, cleaning up for the day at the Zimmers' construction site. Meanwhile, on the new Catholic church grounds, members had gathered together to begin building a rectory. Farmers were plowing, the turkey farmer was rearing chicks, Harvey Wagon asked Maggie Stenner to marry him, and Dr. Ben Burghone was setting up a second doctor's office at the eastern end of Main Street. In the city, steel mill stacks were smoking wildly, and all the citizens of West Emmette and Riverton and northeast Ohio were far away from the volatile discussions going on in Cuba; Washington, DC; and Berlin.

❀ ❀ ❀

Meanwhile, it was dump day. At four o'clock, after Bird and Henry left, Jessie and Charles gathered up the sacks of cans, some flattened boxes, and anything else that didn't fit in their basement incinerator. She opened the front hood of the Corvair and set the bags in the trunk. They called out to Charlotte, who was drying dishes in the kitchen. There was no need to lock the back door of the house, since no houses were locked in West Emmette except at night.

Charles grabbed the berry buckets; then the three piled into the little car and backed onto Meadow Drive, drove to the top, then turned right. They liked this drive to the dump. They drove up Midville Road, already bordered with chicory blooms and clover, away from the Bauer farm and past the Watters' farm. About a mile down the road, at a stop sign, they turned left onto Spade Road, where the route grew more rural, and drove past the Lang and Dewey farms. Then they went up the hill. A steep hill. Up, up the little Corvair pulled, its engine pushing from behind. Jessie sighed in relief at the top of the hill.

There she turned left, drove down a slighter hill, around a bend to another stop sign. A dog barked at a nearby house, and here it was a little remote. A little farther ahead, she turned right into a gravel drive that wound up a steep incline and came out at an open, flat area of dirt and a little hut. No one was there. Jessie pulled up toward the hut, which was on the front edge of the dump: a deep pit in the earth. She told Charlotte to stay in the car. She and Charles unloaded the bags from the trunk, and she stepped toward the edge and thrust each bag down into the pit.

"Okay," Jessie said to Charles. "That's it." She brushed her hands, glad to be done with this chore for another month. The air was heavy with an umbrella of garbage odor. Charlotte pinched her nose in the car, looking at the mounded dirt. As Jessie and Charles walked back to the car, Charles heard a faint whimper sound and looked about. Jessie heard it too. Their eyes arrived together at a box set near the attendant hut at the end of a matted path of grass. They stepped over to it cautiously, peered inside the box, then looked at each other.

Charlotte's eyes followed them from the back seat.

"Wait," Jessie said, catching Charles's arm. He was reaching into the box. Inside was a puppy. "Don't reach in just yet." She looked about. No one was around.

"Did someone leave it?" Charles asked.

"Maybe," Jessie answered. "It looks that way, doesn't it?"

The puppy, a shaggy, dirtied cream-white color with medium length fur and short floppy ears, was alone in a cardboard box with an open top, like from a grocery store. There was no newspaper or blanket inside, no water. No note. Just the puppy and the box. The little dog was curled up in the corner and raised its young, sad eyes in response to their voices.

Charles looked at his mom. Neither needed to say a word. "Yes, Charles," Jessie said to her boy. "I think we should take it home."

Charles picked up the carton, and Jessie opened the back seat car door opposite Charlotte. "What's that?" Charlotte said, surprised. She peered into the box at the puppy, noticing it had a half-white, half-beige face.

"Get out!" Charles yelled at his sister. He would sit in the back seat with the box.

Charlotte crawled over the front seat in haste, and the three— or four—of them started for home.

After coasting back down Spade Road's steep hill and as they approached Midville Road again, Jessie noticed a garage sale sign at a house on the corner and pulled in. She was looking for a desk or vanity for Charlotte's room ... and now maybe some dog items. Yes, there among the furniture sitting on the grass beside the owner's storage garage, was a lovely, old vanity with two drawers and two cupboard doors. It needed to be stripped and refinished, but it was in sound shape. The price was five dollars, and she could do the work herself. She looked about to find the owner standing across the lawn and asked whether he had any dog items.

"No, I'm afraid I don't," he replied. He looked at Jessie, extending a hand. "I don't know you. I'm Bradley Jones." The man was somewhat burly, his dark-brown hair thick in tight swirls across a tan forehead above thick brows.

Jessie shook his hand. "I'm Jessie Conrad." She paused and thought to add, "Jessie Hall Conrad."

"I'm kinda new here," he said. "Well, three years anyway."

"We'll take that vanity there," Jessie said, opening her purse. "It's lovely."

"It belonged to my grandmother," the man explained as Jessie handed him the five dollars. "I just can't keep everything."

As Jessie closed her purse, she noticed a small print or painting propped up in the grass, leaning against a chair behind the man's money box table. It was an oil painting of lavenders and purples— of small flowers in a vase, set ... somewhere. Violets on a table. "Is that for sale?" she asked, pointing to the dusty, unframed, simple work.

"It is," the man said, "but it is ten dollars. It's an original. My grandmother also had it, but I don't know anything about it. It is signed," he added.

"It's really lovely," Jessie said quietly, her glance fixed on the small work of art. But she couldn't afford that. "Just the vanity then," she said softly, gathering up her purse.

The man offered to deliver the vanity, since he had a pickup truck, and Jessie wrote down her address, thanking him again. "I'm right up the road. You can just set it at the garage door if I'm not home."

That evening, they gave the little puppy a good bath in the utility tub in the basement, having found a bowl for water in the cupboard and puppy food at the market. At her desk in her room, Jesse jotted down "puppy" on the calendar for June 17, then opened her wallet and withdrew a one-dollar bill for tomorrow's church offering. She sealed it in a church envelope and put it in her purse on the dresser top for the next morning. One dollar would need to suffice for two, since one had been used toward the vanity. That would leave thirty-four dollars for the rest of the month. She looked in her closet to choose a dress for the next morning, then glanced down at her three pairs of dress shoes. Black, white, or beige. She chose white.

On her desk was the copy of the Billy Graham book Matthew's mother had given her. It was a Bible study, and Jessie looked for the chapter her Sunday school class would be discussing tomorrow morning. She read it until Charles came in.

"What should we name the puppy?" he asked. Charlotte followed him with the dog in her arms. "Hey!" Charles said. "He's not your dog!"

Jessie gently turned her son around with a touch on his arm. "He's *your* dog, Charles, but we need to share the joy, okay? Well, let's think about it, the name, for a couple of days."

"How about Heidi?" Charles said, taking the puppy carefully from his sister.

"I like Bailey!" Charlotte snapped.

"She's a girl!" Charles said. "Bailey's a boy's name."

"Call her Dumpy then!" Charlotte yelled, running out of the room.

Jessie took the puppy on her lap. "She sure is cute, isn't she?" She lightly rubbed the longish hair over the puppy's head and lifted her ears gently in a soft massage. "Your dad would like this puppy, wouldn't he?" Jessie handed the fragile little pup back to Charles. "I like the name Heidi, if that's what you choose."

"How old do you think she is?"

"I don't know. Maybe five, six weeks."

"I wonder how big she'll get."

"I don't know. She looks like a small breed mix."

Charles took Heidi back down the hall and set his dog in her new box in the dinette beside the floor register.

The summer sun hung heavily low in a deep, hot glow of orange moving downward below a dimming blue sky. The township police car moved slowly up Meadow in patrol; officer Raymond, with all four windows down, rested his left arm in its short-sleeved uniform shirt outside the open frame as families throughout town prepared to retire for the night. Another car was also roaming the streets, driven by a young man with no roots or destiny.

In Sunday school the next morning, Charles's class varnished and finished the wooden plaques they had been working on. Charlotte looked at the six-inch square piece of wood on the way back home in the car and asked Charles what it said.

Charles read the words he had carved into the surface with a wood-burning pen. "'All Things Were Made Through Him and Without Him Was Not Anything Made That Was Made.'"

Charlotte listened. "What?" she said with a scrunched nose.

Jessie, driving, held back a snicker. She maybe recognized the wordy Bible verse from the book of John 1; she would check the verse when she got home.

As they pulled into the driveway, Charles asked his mom why Grandpa Hall didn't go to church with them.

"Oh, I don't know," Jessie answered. "Grandpa is a good man. He just ... I guess he considers nature to be his church, Charles."

"Why do we have to go every Sunday?" Charles asked.

"I enjoy it," Jessie replied. "It's the only 'club' I'm interested in."

Back at home, Jessie instructed Charles to get the ladder. "Let's paint a little more. Charlotte, you can help," she said.

"But it's Sunday." Charles knew his mother's rules.

"I know. The neighbors won't know. Let's sneak a little bit more work in on the back porch maybe. You can bring Heidi out with us. You know, we should take Heidi to Vince this week for a look over." Vince Buckner was the village vet, and he happened to live next door to her dad.

The Conrads put on their work clothes. Jessie showed Charles how to scrape the dried putty from the new window frames to prepare for painting, and Charlotte followed with her dad's dusting brush to clear the surface for paint. Jessie worked on the patio garage door, whistling the lively "Money, Marbles and Chalk" song, and love showered down on the three of them.

Down the road, down Midville Road, Bill Watters and Simon Cornwall stood together with their backs to the road, hands on their hips, looking across the twenty front acres of the Watters property. The land, a mile below Meadow Drive and west of the village, was no longer being farmed. It was flat for seven acres, then rose into a treed hillside in the back, where the farmhouse sat.

Simon saw a lake. It wasn't there yet, but Simon wanted it to be and was sharing his vision with Bill. The two had recently met in Simon's business class at the city college. Bill had sold part of his other farmland to the mining company, and he was thinking of starting a small business aside from the acreage he was still farming. Bill had attended Simon's class to learn the economics of such an endeavor; the two got to talking. Simon had visited Hopewell Lake in Lantern County, and it was booming. He thought Clover Township needed a swim lake and thought it would be a good business venture. The two men shook hands at the end of the winter class and were here now to get started.

Simon's right arm swung left and right, pointing to the terrain, sharing his ideas with Bill. Bill nodded, listening, and put his hands in his pockets, half nervous but more so excited. What else could he do with the property?

Simon looked right, then left of the long dirt lane used to enter the farm. "I think the lake should be there," he said. There was lower-lying acreage where one could imagine water.

Bill tried to see it. "Okay," he said. "Who do we talk to?"

"Let's begin with Roger Talmann, owner of Hopewell Lake. I'll invite him over. Could we hunt when he comes? Anyway, he could get us started." Simon looked at his new friend's land, which had once grown pumpkins, berries, and corn but now showed weeds. "Tanser could do the surveying for us. Connor has a bulldozer and dump truck. Talmann could steer us with seeding and soil. Might take us a couple of years, Bill, working summers."

"I've got time," Bill said.

On Main Street, veterinarian Vince Buckner was at that moment talking with Jace Field, who had brought his dog to him for a minor problem. Vince saw animals on any day at any hour. After examining the dog, the vet took the young man's shoulder and, with a bit of confusion, said as they stepped off the porch, "No charge, Jace. I couldn't find anything wrong. Maybe he just ate something disagreeable."

Vince went back inside his house, but Jace lingered on the sidewalk, looking over at Henry's house, staring in a long pause at the quiet frame before returning to his car.

The next morning in the Conrad home, Charlotte asked her mom for help to prepare a cereal box top form to order a bird figurine pictured on the back of the cereal box. She taped one of her hard-earned quarters to the order form, and Jessie wrote the instructed address on a small envelope. Then they took the envelope to the post office, which was a one-room addition built onto the side of Hazel Morgan's house.

Charlotte dropped her envelope in the slot in the wall marked "Mail," then rushed to box 185 to join her mom. Charlotte turned the combination lock dial—left 9, right 15, left 2—and opened the small metal door for her mother to take out the mail. Inside their box lay an envelope from the Social Security

Administration, an envelope from Prudential Insurance, a gas bill, a postcard, a *Ladies' Home Journal* magazine, and another letter from Emma Wolfe.

Mrs. Morgan was at the postal window. "Hi, Charlotte! Hi, Jessie! Happy Monday! Need any stamps today?" she asked, setting down a chocolate bar.

"No, thank you, Hazel. How are you?"

Hazel's husband worked at the dairy nearby and also drove one of the school buses. "We're fine. Are you going to enter a pie at the fair, Jessie?"

"I don't know, Hazel. I haven't given it thought," Jessie replied to her friend and former classmate.

When they returned home, Charles was brushing Heidi in the yard; Heidi spotted a white butterfly moth and now followed it with her little face as it flittered over the lawn.

Charlotte asked, "Mom, can I go down to Becky's house?"

Charlotte's new friend Becky Leskovich lived four lots down on the same side of the street, so it was an easy walk for the girls between homes. A house was being built next door to Becky's. It was in the glorious stage of construction where any curious trespasser could sneak in and walk about the rooms, defined by vertical pillars of raw wood under a new roof. Charlotte's journey to Becky's was across the two lawns and two dirt parcels separating 147 from 135, Becky's house.

Reaching 135 today, she paused cautiously at Becky's side garage door, shyly opened it, then quietly stepped into the garage, which was oddly clean. There were no spots of dirt or oil, and only one pair of shoes rested near the back steps. She knocked on the kitchen door. Mrs. Leskovich came to the screen. She didn't like unexpected company and greeted Charlotte with an uncertain "Hello?"

"Is Becky here?" Charlotte asked carefully.

"Yes, but she's busy. She can't come out right now." Mrs. Leskovich did not invite Charlotte inside.

"Oh ... well, tell her I was here," Charlotte said quietly, taking short steps backward. "Goodbye. Thank you, Mrs. Leskovich," she added.

Charlotte decided to approach the empty house on the lot next door on her own. Charles was usually with her when they explored houses under construction.

The parcel, numbered 139, had already been purchased by a family from Pennsylvania, who would move to Meadow by the end of summer with three more boys. Charlotte's tennis shoes rocked slowly across the barren lot of dirt and stones as she stepped across the backyard area, then stretched her right shoe toward the front end of the board leading upward to the back door. The twelve-inch-wide plank crossed up and over the foundation ditch. She and Charles had walked the plank before. The board sank a little when she reached the middle distance, where a fall would be the worst, and Charlotte rushed to the end of the plank and grabbed the metal knob of the door. Good.

The back door was still unlocked. She turned the knob and pushed the door open into the still, dusty air and stepped inside. The stinging, raw smell of sawdust made her feel at home again and at ease and was, for Charlotte, an invitation to explore. She ventured through the first room of construction and looked at a countertop, where a workman had left a large, dirt-smudged coffee mug. There was a dust-covered, bulky transistor radio beside it. She stepped into the hallway and roamed into the maze of open doorways to what would become bedrooms.

Here was a smaller room. A saw horse was still set up in it. She continued down the hallway length to a tiny, framed space that would probably become a closet. Nails were scattered on the floors here and there.

Suddenly she heard voices outside. Men's voices!

She rushed back through the hallway and found the steps leading to the basement and scampered downward into the dark. Charlotte backed off to the side of the staircase and listened, her heart pounding.

Two men came into the house, talking about something, their voices moving as they crossed the floor above Charlotte and walked into the various rooms. One man was telling the other something about the plaster or drywall or something for the walls. Then they talked for a few minutes about some cabinet work; and as they walked, Charlotte's heart pounded, afraid they would come downstairs. She listened to their heavy steps cross the floor above as they moved, paused, then moved again here and there.

Charlotte looked down at her shoes, where they rested in a small patch of light. There in the chips of wood and sawdust on the set cement was something shiny. She bent down to see what it was. A marble. Someone had dropped a marble. She picked it up and put it in her pocket.

Finally the men's voices grew faint as their footsteps moved back to the entry. Charlotte heard the door open and close above her and then a truck crossing the gravel outside, leaving down the driveway.

Carefully she stepped one by one up the plank stairs, which had no railing yet, and entered the room above. Now someone else was coming up the plank outside! Charlotte ducked back behind the counter. She heard a couple of boys' voices. One was Charles's. The other men had locked the door when they left, so the boys went away. Charlotte waited another minute, then turned the knob, popping the button lock; and with arms stretched out for balance, she glided confidently and gladly down the plank outside.

The afternoon was late. It would be time for supper soon. As Charlotte reached the uneven earth at the foot of the plank and ground, she saw Becky helping her mother take down sheets and towels and aprons from their clothesline. Charlotte didn't call out, nor did Becky wave to her friend, so as not to give her away. Mrs. Leskovich's back was to her. Charlotte sneaked away, running back up across the three yards to her own home.

The supper hour was always five o'clock exactly, the time their father had set. During the school season and summer, the children were to be at the table at five, even when their father had been on the road. Charlotte jumped rope for a few minutes then ran in the back door just in time, threw a little water on her hands, and rushed to her chair.

"What's for supper?" Charles called, out of breath.

"Where were you?" Jessie asked Charles, thinking of the letter she had read from Emma while the children were out.

"With Jackie. We're reading his *Boys' Life*. Mine disappeared."

"I got a letter from Emma Wolfe today. She said their new neighbors have two young daughters. No boys," Jessie said as she set down plates of sloppy joes and a bowl of hot, homemade french fries. Her deep-fried potatoes were always hot, crispy, and full of flavor, lightly salted. Charlotte grabbed the catsup bottle from the refrigerator.

"Sloppy joes! Oh boy!" Charles said. "Where were you?" he said to Charlotte in a demanding tone.

Jessie cautioned her son, "Now don't eat fast. Wait. Let's say grace." She bowed her head. "Bless us, oh Lord, and these Thy gifts, which we are about to receive. Amen." The three always chanted the standard grace together at a different pace.

"Where were you?" Charles persisted.

Charlotte, still sitting on a cushion, reached across the tabletop for the bowl of fries and bumped over her plastic glass of milk.

"Again?" Charles yelled.

The milk ran across the red vinyl tablecloth in an instant stream over to Charles's plate. It ran down a bit off Charlotte's side of the table too, falling in quick, white drops to the floor. Heidi ran over to lap up some of the milk. Jessie grabbed a dish towel and mopped the table quickly, a practice she was used to. "Milk is a wonderful thing, isn't it?" she said, making thoughtful talk to distract from Charlotte's fretting. "Just get some more." She winked at Charlotte. "You need your milk."

"I'm expecting someone after supper," Jessie said quietly while taking the dishcloth over to the sink. "That man Grandpa told me about—for the newspaper job—is coming over. You two can play outside after supper until … seven thirty or eight. Then come in for baths."

"Can we watch *The Andy Griffith Show* tonight?" Charles asked.

"What time is it on?" Jessie said.

"Nine thirty," Charles replied.

"Well, I guess so, after baths."

"Charles, could you write another letter to Walter? You have a lot of news—with the piano…and Heidi."

The family finished eating; Jessie washed the few dishes. Charlotte, standing next to her mother, dried the plates and cups in haste, then ran outside to find Charles, who had run over to the Leigh orchard to climb trees.

Jessie freshened her hair in the bathroom and dabbed some face powder on her nose. Soon the front doorbell rang, and there stood Martin McMillan.

"Your home is lovely, Jessie," Mr. McMillan said as he stepped in and looked about the simple front room with a confident smile. Jessie wondered about his observation of the oblong room. Her eyes followed McMillan's glance toward Matthew's chair near the front door, where his cigarette dish was set on the end table, though Jessie didn't smoke. The old green couch ran along the opposite wall, above which hung four plaster molds of blossom branches representing spring, summer, autumn, and winter.

"Can we sit at the kitchen table?" Mr. McMillan asked.

Martin McMillan was a slight man of medium height. His trousers had been put on early in the morning and were now smudged and wrinkled after a long day at the paper. He looked tired, but his expression still had grace and energy.

"Jessie, I'm sorry about Matthew," Martin said as they walked into the kitchen. "I'm very sorry. Matthew was a fine man. You know we ... we weren't in the same class, but I remember him well."

"Thank you." Jessie said. "I made some coffee. Would you like a cup?"

"Oh yes," he said, relieved. "It's been a long day." He paused, then added, "I saw the news of Matthew's accident come across the wire at the paper."

"Many heard it on the radio that morning," Jessie added. She was thinking of Nelle.

"We did an article in November about the need to regulate hours for truck drivers, Jessie," Martin said gently, wisely. Carefully he added, "Do you think Matthew went off the road due to the fog, or did his schedule tire him, do you think?"

Finally. Finally, someone had said it. "The fog, we believe, Martin," Jessie said, looking into his eyes. "There was a sudden bend in the rural road there in Avalon County. But yes, yes, drivers' hours need to be reviewed and limited. I'm glad to know you wrote an article. I'd like to read it. Thank you for telling me."

Martin McMillan touched Jessie's arm in friendship, then pulled two booklets from his case and set them on the table. "So you're willing to give this a try?" he said to Jessie. "What we need here in the township is for someone to attend the local meetings when they happen. School board. Town council mostly. Any special meeting or the like. For Ingalls, it was about once a week. Often Tuesday or Thursday nights. You go to the meeting, take notes, come home, and write it up. And then you call the city desk at the paper by seven o'clock the next morning. You know we're an afternoon paper, except Sundays, so as long as we have the report before eight, we're good for that day's edition."

"I've never done this before," Jessie said with uncertainty. "I ... I've only worked in a bakery, during the war."

"I know." And Martin McMillan knew Jessie would now need the income. "Ingalls is moving to another department at the paper, but she is available to help you get started."

"Well ..."

"You will do fine though, I think. Look at your father. I'm sure some of the historian is in you too. He maybe can help you too. And so can I. Read these two books. They explain the business."

Jessie flipped open the top page of the yellow booklet titled *AP Stylebook*. Inside, on the credit page, Mr. McMillan had written in bold pencil, "This, roughly, is our paper's style. There are some exceptions." The first sentence of the book's introduction said, "This book is for the guidance and benefit of those engaged in preparing material for newspapers."

Martin took a sip of coffee. "The first meeting you'll need to report isn't until August seventeenth, I think. Or the fourteenth. Just go to the meeting, take a notepad and pencil, take notes and names, and tell me what was discussed and decided. You've read Ingalls's articles—a few maybe since you've been home. Well, anyway, here are two of them." He set the clipped newspaper strips down on the books. "You'll do fine, I'm sure. These books tell you everything. And here." He reached for a brochure and added it to the table. "I'm sure you understand the structure of a township, but this Ohio publication explains its history and makeup and purpose. Good to keep in mind."

He took another sip of coffee and looked at Jessie, who quietly stared at the booklets on the table. He said, "How are you doing, Jessie?"

She raised her eyes to his with appreciation and replied, "Well, the Walkers next door have been a blessing. Luther comes over to help us lift things and repair things when we need help. Chalky—Raymond Jones—has been amazing. Just amazing." And here her eyes teared up slightly, but she ably held the tears back. "And my dad. And Charles is becoming handy too. He is trying to step up and be the man of the house. And ... thank God for Social Security."

"You know," Martin said, eyebrows raised, "the paper is planning a feature about Social Security this winter. The program is twenty-five years old. Maybe we'll call you to talk or help. Anyway, I'm glad you have that assistance."

"Matthew was a veteran, you know."

"I know."

"We'll get by. This job will help. Thank you, Martin."

"We need you!" He smiled. "You might enjoy this, Jess!" Though so tired, he spoke with sincerity and a pump of joy. He added, "Do you have a typewriter?"

Suddenly Jessie felt the idea was unrealistic and that Martin had made a crazy mistake in approaching her. "No," she replied gravely.

"I have an old small one. It's nice. Light. You can have it." He winked. "It's in my trunk." He saw she was worried. "And I'll ask Ingalls to go to the first meeting with you, okay? It will make it easier, but you do the writing. Call me. My number is in the front of that booklet."

After Martin left, Charles ran into the house and went to his mom in the living room by the front door. "Mom! Jackie asked if I could come over and play marbles and trade baseball cards. He wanted to know if I could sleep out over there tonight too," he said in a quick breath.

Jessie smiled. This one was easy. Their backyards were adjacent to each other and she would be able to keep an eye on them too.

Charles grabbed his sleeping bag and marble bag, and ran to the door. Heidi yapped excitedly alongside him. "No, girl. You should stay here. I'll be back in the morning," he told his dog. Noticing that his marble bag seemed lighter, he stepped back into the kitchen, pulling open the fabric pouch. "Where's my shooter?" he yelled into Charlotte's face. Charlotte had quietly reentered the kitchen a minute after Mr. McMillan left.

"I don't know!" she yelled back.

"Here," Jessie said. "Wait a minute." She walked down the hallway to the end closet and pulled out a box. She took something from it and stepped back to Charles, who had followed her. "Here, use this." She handed him a different, opaque white shooter.

"Wow," he said in a small drawl of admiration, turning the big marble over in his hand. "This is a beaut!" And he turned and ran out the door.

Jessie went to find Charlotte, who had gone to her mother's desk with her coloring book and scrapbook. Charlotte, sitting before the open coloring book with a gold crayon in hand, had reached for her mother's snow globe with the boy figurine inside and was turning it upside down and right side up again, watching the snow fall within.

She could use a desk soon, Jessie thought.

Charlotte resumed coloring a lamp in the picture. Only special objects were colored gold with the coveted crayon.

"C'mon Charlotte," Jessie said to her daughter. "It's you and me tonight. Let's have some popcorn."

Charlotte brought her coloring book, scrapbook, and glue jar to the kitchen. Jessie opened the hi-fi cabinet and put a record on the player. The lively, familiar "tick tock tick tock" opening notes of the "Green Door" song filled the house.

"Green Door ... What's that secret you're keepin'?" Jim Lowe sang.

Jessie and Charlotte grabbed hands and danced into a circle, making up their own little jig. "Green Door! What's that popcorn you're poppin'?" they yelled, changing the lyrics.

Jessie went to the kitchen, took the new Jiffy Pop popcorn container down from the cupboard, and turned on the gas stove flame. "Oh boy!" Charlotte gasped, running to the stove. As the record continued, the song's steady beats began to compete with the heating popcorn leaping in its foil dome, and the two girls stood watch at the stove burner while Jessie gently shook the wire handle and the foil pan began to rise and grow into a rounded crown filled with popped corn.

At the table, Jessie gave Charlotte the most recent comics and news magazine from the Sunday newspaper for clipping pictures and cartoons. Charlotte found a Blondie comic, got a piece of paper, and tried to draw her own version of it with her crayons. She used the bright-red crayon to color Dagwood's shirt, blue for his chair, and green to match Blondie's dress. Yellow for her hair.

Jessie opened the small paperback book Mr. McMillan had left for her. It was about five-by-seven inches in size, bound in a light-gold, puckered paper cover, with the title *AP Stylebook*. The words "The Associated Press" were on the bottom in a brown band.

Inside, on the first page, was a credit to a "G. P. Winkler" with the Associated Press's address at 50 Rockefeller Plaza, New York 20, N.Y." Dated 1960.

Also inside the cover was a loose piece of short, light-brownish paper with some typing on it. The county name was typed in the top left. Then centered about an inch from the top was the word *Special* in parentheses. Then: "West Emmette, August 14—All stories start this way—about 2 inches from the top," Martin had typed, and he had marked this measurement darkly in heavy pencil with two arrows pointing down from the top. Then there was her name, on the next line: "Mrs. Jessie Conrad." Then he began:

"The deadline for the county edition of The Post—in which copy from West Emmette and Clover Township and the school district appears—is 10:15 a.m. Monday through Saturday."

Mr. McMillan had typed that instruction on this separate page, on the thin newsprint paper. He continued, "If some big news event occurs after the deadline, the story can be used in later editions of the paper, so don't hesitate to call at any time if it's important. For that, you would ask for the State Desk." One word of that sentence had been crossed out in a heavy scratch with a bracket drawn over it.

Charlotte took out a crayon to match the color of her mother's new book, and she colored the dog she had just drawn the same pale, yellowish tan.

After the next lines of phone numbers, Martin had typed, "If mailing a story, mail your copy in plenty of time. It is no good to us late. In case you hear of major crashes anywhere in the area, or fires, drownings, etc., give us a call IMMEDIATELY. This sometimes enables us to send a photographer and reporter straight to the scene ... but you keep gathering info until we inform you someone else is on the way."

Jessie wondered whether a reporter had rushed to the scene where Matthew's truck had overturned in the ditch.

Charlotte and Jessie nibbled on the popcorn, and Jessie sipped her root beer, looking into the book's chapters about capitalization of military titles, world regions, names of flowers, and quotations. Then came abbreviations, rules, punctuations, numerals.

"Gee," she said to Charlotte, "I feel like I'm going to school."

"Good, Mommy!" Charlotte said, dropping some kernels. "We can be in school together this year!" Then with a small yawn, Charlotte put down her crayons. "When does school start? I can't wait!"

"Well, not until after Labor Day, in early September after the fair."

"The fair?" Charlotte said. "Do you think Charles is asleep yet?" she added sleepily. The kitchen clock showed the time of nine thirty.

"I doubt it," Jessie answered. "Let's watch *The Andy Griffith Show*." The two girls enjoyed some television, then Charlotte asked again, "Do you think Charles is asleep now?"

"I don't know," Jessie answered. "Let's look out the window."

They couldn't see the tent from the window, so they ventured out onto the back porch into the summer night to listen and look across the side yard. Jessie carried Heidi to the grass. The tent, visible to the right from their patio behind a couple of bushes at the back of the Walkers' corner yard, still glowed from a golden light within. The mom and daughter could hear Jackie's voice—a pitch all critters in the woods would be alerted by.

Jessie glanced over at the Walker home and could see Gloria looking out her kitchen window. Jessie stepped to the side of the back porch, where Gloria could see her in the dim patio bulb light and waved a hello. Gloria waved back.

Jessie scooped up their little dog, and she and Charlotte quietly went back into the house, leaving the song of night crickets behind as the door swung slowly toward them on its spring. Jessie left the door unlocked and the little lamp on the kitchen counter lit, should Charles wish to come in, then she and Charlotte brushed their hair and teeth together in the bathroom.

Charlotte watched her mother wash her face and open the jar of cold cream. "Can I put some on too?" she asked.

"Well, sure, but you'll probably find it to be greasy for your young skin, so just a little bit." Jessie placed a few sponge curlers in her daughter's hair and rubbed a little anti-itch ointment on two fresh mosquito bites.

In the bedroom, Charlotte reached for her stuffed dog, Spot, who felt so real with comforting eyes and warm, soft fur. She held it to her little chest so Spot could share the heartbeat through her pajamas. She asked her mom whether she could sleep in her room.

"That would be fun," Jessie said. "What book should we read tonight?"

Charlotte went to the book box. Her name and Charles's name were carved in a beautiful scroll on each side. She would have that to keep, with the little rocking chair and the magnificent bent-wood dresser her dad had also made, through the years to come. The great cedar chest was in her mom's room.

Charlotte's little fingers flipped forward through the books, some with gold bindings and others with green or black colors, which were already worn on the corners. She skipped past *The Little Train That Saved the Day*, *The Lone Ranger*, and two other books; she came to *I See the Sea*. When she took it to her mom's room, Jessie said, "Aren't you a little tired of that book?"

Charlotte looked down at the little girl in her red swimsuit on the book cover, crouching on the sand with her beach pail against a sea-green and blue horizon. She wasn't tired of the story and pictures at all. Should she be?

"How about your dad's book of poems?" It was among Charlotte's books in the box. "Or better yet, how about you read to me?" Jessie said. "Get your farm book, the *Milk for You and Me* book." And the two propped themselves up with pillows to read, turning to the first page.

"'This is your book,'" Charlotte read slowly, while the pedals of the clover flowers out in the kitchen on the windowsill closed for the night. "'You may read it. It tells a story. Read about the cows. They give milk. It is a book for you and me.'"

Soon it was July, and temperatures reached 90 degrees on some days. On Saturday, July 22, the persistent, soft rattle of summer crickets rocked the morning awake, their chirping moving gently in waves up the backyard from the woods.

At ten o'clock sharp, Mary Bauer came back to 147. This time she came to the back door, handing to Jessie a large basket. Jessie nodded in partnership, and after she took the basket to the basement, the two women moved quickly to the living room for the children's piano lessons. Charles would go first, so he could get outside to join his friends. Charlotte, dressed in a pink, sleeveless cotton blouse with matching shorts, had her blonde hair, curled from the curlers, tied up in a ponytail. She sat on the couch with her mom and listened to Charles's mistakes. Mary instructed Charles to play the C-major scale to warm up and then the right hand of the "Tick-Tack-Toe" song on page thirteen. She stopped him after four measures.

Jessie picked up her sewing basket to mend some socks. She grasped the light bulb in her left hand, with the cotton sock stretched tightly over it, stitching a gaping hole with her strongest white thread.

"What is that note, Charles?" Mary said, pointing to the song measure in the booklet.

"An F," he responded.

"That's right, but what type of note is it?"

"A quarter note."

"Yes, and what is that symbol?" She was pointing to the sharp symbol, called an "accidental."

"A sharp."

"And where is that key?"

Charles looked down at the keyboard and found the black key to the right of the white F key.

"Yes," Mary said. "Okay, let's try again, and I'll count for you."

Charles placed his hands on the keys.

"No," Mary said, "hold them up this way." She pulled his boyish hands up and out into a curl that looked unnatural, and he tried to hold them in that shape. But it made him pound the keys even more awkwardly.

Charles could follow the notes and proceeded to slowly play out the song, but he struck the keys hard, as if trying to make them stick in the down position. Mary worked with him for the next twenty minutes and reminded him to think about the song and to listen for the melody. She asked him to play the G-major preparatory drill a few times, checked his theory book, marked his next lesson in their notebook, then let him go. As Charles sprang to the front door, Jessie called after him. "Playground?"

"Yep!" Charles called back, and off he went on his bicycle down the street, with his ball glove dangling in sway on the handlebar.

"Okay, Charlotte." Mary smiled. "Your turn. Let's look at your lesson."

While Charlotte moved happily to the piano bench, Mary flipped through the John Schaum Book A to page ten. "Let's see how you do, Charlotte. This is a cute song, isn't it?"

As Charlotte began to play the simple melody, the phone rang in the kitchen. Jessie answered it quietly. "Oh, hello, Sally," she said. It was Sally from church, and as she began to speak, Jessie reached for a pencil. "Okay … um-hmm …" Her pencil scribbled quickly in response to what Sally was telling her about the church tent planned for the fair. Maybe she could use this call and information for a practice newspaper story, she thought.

When Charlotte's lesson ended, Jessie explained the call to Mary.

"Our church has a stand there too," Mary said. "Well, Jessie, are you going to show Charlotte what I brought with me?"

Jessie and Charlotte's eyes met at the same moment— Charlotte's with curiosity and Jessie's with love. Jessie took Charlotte's hand, and the women walked to the kitchen. Jessie retrieved the large basket, and she carried it carefully into the kitchen, setting the basket on the floor rug near the sink. It made a noise.

Charlotte lifted the light cloth draped across the top, and inside lay a tiny, multi-colored kitten! "Oh! Mrs. Bauer! Oh!" Charlotte began to reach into the basket but pulled her arms back, not sure how to pick it up. "Oh! It's so pretty, Mom!"

"She's yours, Charlotte," her mother said. "She's a calico, they're called, because they have three colors in their fur. Black, orange, and white." Jessie paused. "Sort of like our school colors actually," she said to Mary, both women loving the moment.

Charlotte reached again for the basket but was still unsure how to pick up the kitten. "How do I get her out?" Charlotte said to Mrs. Bauer.

Mary reached into the basket with her traveled hands, colored from the sun and experienced with the births of baby cows, goats, and sometimes puppies. She lifted the tiny, meowing ball of fur with two pointed ears onto the kneeling lap of Charlotte Conrad. It was, as life would live out, the first gift of many which would be given between the two friends.

Jessie dabbed a tissue to her eye and paid Mary for the piano lessons.

"Next week you can let me know what you name her, Charlotte," Mary said before leaving. "She's a girl kitten." To Jessie she said, "Are you going to enter a pie, Jessie?"

Jessie had to think back a moment to the phone call. "At the fair? Well, I'll bake a pie for the church tent," she answered.

"No, I mean are you going to enter one of your pies for a ribbon?"

Here sat as surely as their heavy ovens the great unspoken contest. Mary had long been considered the best pie maker in the village and even the township. She had access to fresh cream and eggs for custard pies, and she tapped her father's orchard for fruit. Mary was skilled and practiced, and she could whip up any pie with ease, and they were good.

But Jessie had worked in a bakery during the war and had her own family recipes and a natural knack none of her friends could match. In her youth her father had had grape vines in the backyard, and Jessie had learned how to make concord grape pie from the woman who cared for her and Ethel. Jessie had perfected it all with a born talent for crust.

"No," Jessie answered, walking her friend to the door. "Just a pie for the tent."

When Mary left, Jessie and Charlotte set about making provisions for the kitten. When Charles came home, Charlotte's eyes grew wide when she watched her brother for a reaction to her kitten. "What?" he yelled. "A kitten? Are you kidding?"

Charlotte pulled the kitten close to her young neck and shoulder. Her hair ribbon attracted the kitten's attention.

"What about Heidi?" Charles asked his mother, calming down, then looking more interested at the kitten. He smiled to Charlotte. "Can I pet her?" He reached out to touch the kitten's head. Charlotte held her breath.

"Heidi and the kitten will learn to get along," Jessie said. "They might even enjoy each other's company." The three Conrads closed the doors and chose a space for the kitten to become acclimated, away from Heidi. While Charlotte played with the kitten, dragging her hair ribbon across the floor, Charles took Heidi outside, and Jessie made dinner.

At the dinner table, Jessie changed the subject to talk about the fair. It would be their first September in West Emmette. She poured tomato juice into their glasses and placed a casserole and steaming sweet corn on the table. Sweet corn crops were coming in early, and this was the first of the season. Mary had brought six ears of their corn. "There is a big fair in the county here, called the Perch County Fair, and it opens on the Thursday of the last week of summer vacation, before Labor Day. It runs five days before you go back to school," Jessie told them.

"What was that Mrs. Bauer said about a pie?" Charlotte asked.

"Well, this fair … it is one of the largest fairs in Ohio." Charles was all ears. "I went to it with Aunt Ethel and Grandpa when I was young … and your dad and I enjoyed it too before we moved to Columbus. Anyway, it is a lot of fun, and you'll want to take your allowance with you."

Jessie saw Charlotte's expression twist into panic. Charles was way ahead of her in allowance. "Mom, can I dust for you tomorrow?" Charlotte said urgently.

Jessie smiled. "Don't worry, Charlotte. I'll make sure you can earn a little more money before the fair."

"What do they have there?" Charles asked.

"Well, they have rides—like the merry-go-round and Ferris wheel. And they have games. And horse shows. Lots of animals and food … corn dogs and cotton candy."

"And what about that pie thing?" Charlotte asked.

"Well, women can enter pies or cakes or cookies and things … pickles and canned fruit and such, to be judged by some judges. They taste them and decide which one deserves a blue ribbon."

"Oh, Mom, you should enter a pie," Charles said. "Which kind? Elderberry?"

"No, peach!" Charlotte called out.

That Wednesday, Ethel said, "Grape pie, Jessie. That's what you should enter."

"I don't know," Jessie answered her sister. Ethel had stopped in after getting her hair done. "Your hair looks nice." She admired Ethel's sprayed style.

"I couldn't get a perm today. Full moon, you know," Ethel said, patting her puffed white bob.

"I think I shouldn't enter a pie," Jessie countered. "Besides, I have enough to do, Ethel." She took Ethel's arm. "Come and see the vanity I refinished for Charlotte." Jessie led her sister to the basement. "I have one more coat of varnish to apply, and it will be ready for Charlotte's room before school starts."

Ethel admired the vanity and liked the rose-brown wood stain. "Gee, what nice drawer pulls ... and carving on the doors," Ethel said. "And who's this?" she said with delight, bending down to pet the new kitten, who appeared from under the vanity and rubbed Ethel's ankle, then fell onto her shoes. Ethel reached down to pick her up. "What did you decide to name her?"

"Lucy," Jessie said with delight.

"I like it," Ethel said. She nearly added, *Your family's growing* but thought better of it. Holding the kitten to her cheek, Ethel followed Jessie back upstairs to the kitchen. "The prize is five dollars."

"What?" Jessie said.

"The pie prize, at the fair."

"Oh. But Mary is being very generous to Charlotte and Charles with the piano lessons, and I really am grateful." Jessie poured her sister a cup of tea.

"So? What does that have to do with your entering a pie?" Ethel said, setting the kitten down on the kitchen floor. Heidi ran up to sniff Lucy's nose and tiny mouth; the cat hissed back.

"Well, Mary has won several times, hasn't she? I don't want to compete."

"Because you'll beat her."

Jessie sighed with appreciation. "I don't know about that."

"Well, I do!" Ethel gave her sister a little hug, then reached for one of the raisin cookies on the counter. Ethel wasn't as thin as Jessie. "So are you working in the church booth? I am." Ethel sipped from her cup at the table. "When will you begin to work for the paper?"

"In August. Next month."

"What's first?"

"A school board meeting. I'm nervous."

"Well, Daddy will be there. You'll be fine."

"That's a pretty necklace, Ethel," Jessie said, noticing a new chain—the long kind coming into fashion.

"Well, it's a good thing I bought this ribbed top, because otherwise I wouldn't have bought this necklace!" Ethel beamed.

The sisters laughed. Ethel laughed with her entire body, and her sudden bursts of inhales over a quickly stiffened posture topped with bejeweled, glistening eyes always made Jessie happy.

"Here," Ethel said, sliding a paper bag across the table to Jessie, her eyes now full of love. "This is for you. It's a scrapbook for your newspaper stories."

That evening Jessie read more from the instructional books Martin had given her. She reread the preface by Donald Ross of the 1958 *Newspaper Correspondent's Manual.* "A primary purpose of newspapers is to inform readers about the happenings of the day," it began. "Presumably every man, woman and child read at least some portion of a newspaper with considerable regularity. What they read influences their actions and their lives."

There was a chapter in the manual for "Church and Club News," and Jessie turned to page twenty. "Correspondents should be alert to the possibility of reporting church, welfare and club news in a wider concept than is usual. The writer of this news does not report as does the secretary of an organization, who records all detail in a running account." *Where does it say how to begin?* Jessie wondered, looking ahead in the booklet. "Correspondents are urged to form lists of organizations and the spokesmen for them. Priests and pastors should be contacted."

Page twenty-four was about "Schools," and page twenty-five was about "Farm News." "Interesting," Jessie whispered, reading the helpful paragraphs. "It is here that youngsters are learning in projects directed by the Future Farmers of America, the Future Homemakers of America and the 4-H," the book said.

"Conservation measures to provide trees, better pasture and crop lands and improved production methods are stories which teach others."

What would Matthew think of my new reporting job? Jessie wondered. Ripples of thought about the night when she had lost him still appeared faintly through her days. *Was it the fog?* Jessie wondered again. *Was it the fog?* She thought of her husband's semitrailer truck lying on the side of the road on the bend like a beached whale.

She turned the pages of the booklets. She could find no instruction for writing the first sentence. She gathered together the sample newspaper clippings from Martin and others she had saved, and she put them on the table next to her notebook. She took up her pencil and wrote, "The women of Old Clover Reformed Church will again ..." She turned her pencil upside down, held the pencil shaft midlength, and erased her first sentence with short strokes. *No*, she thought and then wrote, "Old Clover Reformed Church will again host a food tent at the Perch County Fair." She erased the word *again* and wrote "once again."

Henry M. Hall was at his desk too, logging additional notes for his printed history of the township, which he had completed in 1939. He had heard that Roberta Edwards was beginning to pen a second history of contemporary families and more about the businesses in town. But his pencil kept turning to words about Canada, his camping trips, and the pages he had written reflecting on his time with Indian Jim. He opened his gray binder to the fifth chapter and reviewed his script.

> The brilliance of the July moon lighting up the heavens, reflecting its multiple rays upon the surface of the lake in Mashegama, was second

only to the crystal light of the starlight, such as is
only found in the high altitudes of the far north.

In this wild terrain the moon looked down upon
a most peaceful camp scene as four white men
and three Indians sat around a campfire on a small
island perhaps two miles from the mainland.

Indian Steve, the companion of Indian Jim, our
guide of the expedition, had just returned from
a journey of some seventy miles, bringing flour
and bacon in his satchel, which every Indian scout
always had hidden away for emergencies in the
rough regions of his homeland.

Henry read past his paragraphs about fishing for great northern
pike to the page where the party entered the maple woods the
following morning. "The entrancing beauty of trees has ever been
the inspiration for verse and song. Their stately majesty and quiet
peaceful solicitude have long made them the haven of refuge for
the weary and distressed."

Henry looked ahead to the notes he had made about Jim's
warnings. "When vast areas of forest trees are destroyed, such
change interrupts the course of nature in the proper distribution
of moisture. With the passing of the forests, rain can only fall
harshly upon bare ground, from which has passed away the root
systems, moss, ferns, and habitations of the creatures who once
abided there, all with a task to perform in the loosening of the
soil in the greatest and most efficient water system in the world."

❈ ❈ ❈

Henry pushed his chair back and paced over to the large Waterbury Regulator clock beside the ornate Gustav Becker clock, looking into her face. He paused there a long minute, studying the movement of the scrolled iron second hand, listening to her deep heartbeat, the heavy brass disc pendulum swinging left, right, left, right. *Why did I have that dream?* he wondered. Returning to his desk, he took out from the left drawer a notebook that held some of the magazine and newspaper reviews of his book and the correspondence of his "automatic mailbox" sketch and patent application; then he searched for his formula for cleaning gun barrels. *There it is.* He stopped, picking up his pencil. "Alcohol, 1.5 oz., blue vitriol, 1 oz., nitric acid, ¾ oz." Henry listed the seven ingredients on a scratch of paper for tomorrow's task of cleaning his guns, while Jace Field drove by and down Main Street on his way to a new job of sweeping floors at the grocery.

CHAPTER 6

Twenty steps to the ditch. Twenty-seven steps from the left side to the right side. Jessie could hear Charles counting as she watched her son mowing the young grass on the front lawn, which had filled in nicely since the April seeding.

With her hand tool, Jessie moved from the petunias at the front of the house to the row along the back side to trim the grass along the flower beds. The morning air smelled like tea. *Tea and bark,* Jessie thought. She could see the Queen Anne's lace and cattails swaying gently along Bauer Lane as Mr. Bauer's tractor began to comb the cornfield beyond their yard across Midville Road.

It was August 14, the day of the school board meeting, and Jessie was nervous. At the lunch table, the picnic table on the back patio, Charlotte was cutting the box top coupon from the cereal box she and Charles had emptied that morning. She now had three coupons and enough to send to the cereal company for her second bird figurine. She cut the order form from the box bottom, Jessie filled it in for her, then Charlotte taped a quarter to the cardboard form once more. Jessie addressed the envelope and gave Charlotte a four-cent stamp. Charles turned off the mower, closed the gas valve, and pushed the mower into the garage.

"Hurry up, Charlotte!" Charles called to his sister. "C'mon! The lists are up!"

Just then Jackie ran over to the porch from his house. "Ready, Charles?" Let's go!" he called. "Today's the day!"

Charles said, "Charlotte wants to mail something at the post office on our way."

"But that's past the school!" Jackie complained, noticing the sugar cookies on the picnic table. Jessie nodded to him to take one.

"I know," Charles said. "But it will only add a couple of minutes."

"I'm ready," Charlotte said, licking the envelope.

The three hurried to the garage, and Charlotte and Charles pulled their bikes out from the side wall. Jessie watched. Today was the day the class lists would be posted on the outside of the school doors. "Be careful!" she called to them. "Wait! Will the bookmobile be there today?"

The three kids set their bikes back down and dispersed back to their rooms, grabbed their library books, then returned to their bikes, placing the books in their baskets.

"Watch for cars," Jessie added.

There were few cars on the road in the village during the day; rightly so, for bicycles had the right of way in the summer. It seemed an inherited right or ownership that the youth could sail anywhere at any time on their bicycles about town until dark.

Charlotte's bike was her brother's old bike. So it was a boy's bicycle, but she had learned to push off and swing her right leg over the bar. At least the bike was red.

Jackie and Charles rode fast down Meadow. Charlotte trailed behind. They rode past Becky's house; she wasn't outside. As they neared the shortcut to the back of the school property, which was behind Cap's house on Meadow, Jackie forgot they had to go to the post office first and turned right off the road onto the path, entering the beaten grass lane they used to cut through to the playground and the back of the school.

"Hey, Jack!" Charles called out to stop him. But just then Susan Bachus was coming down her driveway on her bike across the street.

"Charlotte!" Susan called out, seeing her friend.

Charles said to Charlotte, "How about you and Susan ride to the post office together and meet us at the school?"

"Okay," Charlotte said, and Charles turned his bike in a quick loop, entered the shortcut behind Jackie, and peddled fast, standing up above the seat, pushing hard to catch up with his friend.

"Hi, Susan!" Charlotte called. Susan's bicycle was pink and had a pink and white basket with plastic flowers on it.

"Are you going to check the lists?" Susan asked excitedly.

"Yes, but will you ride to the post office with me first?" Charlotte asked.

"Okay!" And on the two girls went, continuing down the straight stretch of Meadow Drive, which would bend at the end to join Main Street, where they would turn right at the sidewalk and ride past Emmette's gas station and five houses to Mrs. Morgan's house and the post office.

Charlotte ran inside, dropped her envelope into the mail slot; then she rushed back out to Susan and her bike. Charlotte kicked the stand back, gave the bike a push, threw her right leg up over the back tire and bar, and pushed hard on the right peddle to get it going. Standing to get some speed, she pulled back on the black plastic handle grips and pushed both pedals around and around hard; after passing three more houses, they were at the front entrance of the school.

The two girls hurried their bikes around the side of the building on the light gravel drive to the blacktop pad, which ran the back length of the building. There were two hopscotch frames painted there and a basketball net farther down. Out on the field beyond in the grass was a baseball diamond—right behind Rooster's house—and a row of two swing sets with good, high swings. There was a tall sliding board and a set of three teeter-totters off to the left near the fence bordering the Zimmers' storage building. The Zimmer brothers and Luther had made the teeter-totters with industrial pipe frame and three solid oak boards mounted with staple-shaped iron handles. The seat portions at the ends of the boards easily held two bodies, if desired.

But the groups of kids who were there that morning weren't on the playground or ball field or even in the bookmobile, parked nearby. All the bikes were dropped on the blacktop near the water fountain on the brick wall at the locked back doors of the school.

On the two building doors, which were oddly dark and motionless in the summertime, were taped thirteen sheets of paper. On them were the lists of students' names and whose rooms they were assigned to for the new school year.

There was one sheet for kindergarten, two for first grade, two for second grade, and so on up to sixth grade. Charles and Jackie were already going into fourth grade, and they leaned in with Bobby and Mitch, who were there too to see which teacher they had.

Charles glanced back and noticed Charlotte's arrival when Susan and Charlotte set their bikes down and joined hands to approach the group.

"I hope we have the same teacher," Susan said.

"I hope so too," Charlotte said, crossing her fingers.

The girls scanned the papers. There was first grade … then a page down were the "Second Grade" lists. There were two rows of names typed in vertical columns. The left page was titled "Mrs. Crosby," and the right page was titled "Mrs. Shore." They had heard good things about Mrs. Shore, so their eyes moved there first.

"Anderson, Arnold, Bachus, Bellweather, Brady, Boldman, Carolle, Conrad!" The girls' index fingers moved down the list to their names.

"Charlotte!" Susan exclaimed. "We're in the same room!"

"I know! I see! Yay! Yay! We're in! We're together!" Charlotte clapped.

Susan, stepping back, whispered to her friend, "And Steve's in our class too!"

Just then, Sebastian and Kenny rode up to the group. As they set their bikes down with all the others, they noticed Susan and Charlotte and softly muttered "Hi" as they approached the doors. Charlotte and Susan giggled a little, and as they went to their bikes to walk them over to the bookmobile, Charlotte flashed back in memory to riding in the back seat of their family car with Walter and Charles in Columbus and being driven home by her mother and father from her ballet recital. It was raining as they drove through the unfamiliar city streets; the rain accentuated the traffic lights and colors of the bright city sidewalks, which flashed by through the car windows that night. Charlotte had been nervous about the recital, but she got through her performance. She even liked it. In the car, Walter whispered something to Charlotte and handed her a ring.

"Are you going to the fair?" Susan asked Charlotte as they gathered their books.

"Yes!" she answered. "I've saved two whole dollars, and I'm going to buy … something," Charlotte said, setting the bike stand. "Are you going?"

"I think so," Susan said.

Charlotte turned her attention to deciding which books to look for today. Another Dr. Seuss book maybe and a book about rocks. She could barely wait to look at the shelves inside—all the colorful spines of books, the labeled shelves—where the smell was ... of a different world. The girls had to step high to the raised metal stair as they grasped the hand rail leading into the mobile library.

Charles, Jackie, and Bobby left the schoolyard to return to Charles's house to continue work on the path they were creating through the woods at the back of the Conrad yard. They had already beaten a sort of footpath, mainly at the forest's wooded edge between some ash and maple trees, where the earth was less rooted and a little drier. The entry was immediately cooling and canopied, and within a few feet, their footpath turned a little to the right, then to the left over a large tree root that created a small ramp. Overhead, here and a bit farther in were some sturdy hanging vines, where the path ended, and the boys stopped there to grasp a vine and swing, sort of like monkeys. Today they needed to choose a direction to continue the path inward, for they wanted to establish a bike route.

Bobby had a rake, and Jackie had a short-handled shovel his dad had let him borrow. Charles took their rake to the woods too.

"My dad's comin'," Jackie bragged. "He said he'd help us today a little. He's on vacation!"

Sure enough, soon they heard Mr. Walker, who had seen the boys' bikes, dropped at the entrance to the woods. He had a wheelbarrow, a sickle, a shovel, and some yard gloves.

"Hey, boys," he said, finding them a few yards in. He looked at the work they had already done. "This looks pretty good!" He handed each of them some old cotton gloves. "Wear these, and ... do you all know what poison ivy looks like?"

"Yeah, I do!" Bobby shouted. He quickly looked down at the forest floor under his feet. There were none of the three-leaf shiny plants nearby. Mr. Walker surveyed the treed woodland ahead with its mass of young and old trees and fallen branches and carpet of moss and old leaves. "Where are you boys goin' with this?"

Charles stood back and listened. "Well," Jackie said to his dad with quick confidence, "we thought we'd go that way." And he pointed toward an area of growth that let some filtered light down onto it.

"What is your plan?" Mr. Walker said. The boys quietly glanced at each other, then looked around into the wild growth of canopied darkness. Bobby withdrew the metal flashlight in his pocket.

"Well," Mr. Walker went on, smiling, "you've done a darn good job so far." The entrance the boys had created into the woods had been raked, and the dirt had settled into a charming matted base. "When you rake the stones and twigs and bark back, do you want to set them at the side of the path to create a sort of border?"

"Not really, Dad, because we want to ride our bikes back here," Jackie said.

"Okay, good thinking then. Well, let's just continue to rake. And I'll cut a little where it's too thick and dig where it's too rocky. Charles, if I leave a hole, you fill it in and smooth it out. Over the weeks, as we get a little farther in, the more you ride your bikes through, the more it will roll out the path."

The man and boys got to work. They raked for two hours, slowly choosing the forward path wherever the trees and earth invited them, trying to keep it straight enough for bikes but interesting enough for surprise.

When they came to a section of stray young trees of new growth and some old broken trunks that blocked progress, Mr.

Walker called to Jackie to go back out to the entrance and get his small saw. "Don't run with it, Son. You know the rule."

"Blade side down," Jackie repeated.

Charles remembered that rule too.

While the children were out, Jessie had prepared an early supper and dressed for the evening meeting. With some anxiety, she watched the kitchen clock hands move into the evening hour. Supper was now over, and Jessie awaited the arrival of Bridget, who would babysit while she was at the board meeting. Bridget was Jackie's older sister; she was sixteen and in high school. It was a perfect convenience. She was a nice girl, she lived right next door, and she was a Walker.

Jesse recalled that when she had moved into the home on Meadow last December, Luther had offered to install the cherry paneling on the side living room wall as soon as he had time. The beautiful wood was to have been placed in their new home in Columbus. Matthew had just purchased and finished the paneling before the accident. Jessie had moved the wood here. It was one of the few reminders she could live with.

She kept only the one photo of the four of them on display in the house, which now rested on the piano top next to Charles and Charlotte's framed school portraits. Displaying only a few photos of Matthew was one of the suggestions the counselor at church had recommended. And the short afternoon nap, which she did find helpful.

Bridget knocked at the side kitchen door. It was 6:15.

"Hello, Mrs. Conrad!" she called through the screen. Heidi barked. "It's only me, Heidi," she said to the small, fluffy dog through the door screen.

"Hi, Bridget! Come in!" Jessie said toward the doorway.

Bridget carried a small stack of books, a tote bag, and purse. Bridget's mother, Gloria, a Lutheran, had told Jessie that Bridget was dating a Catholic boy, something she was uneasy about. It had been only five years now since Holy Rosary Church was built, and already there were one hundred Catholic families in the township. Before the new church building had been built, those families drove to Hunter or Benton to attend church, but now the town seemed to be blooming Catholics.

"Is your mom going to the meeting tonight?" Jessie asked.

"Yeah," Bridget answered, moving gum to the side of her cheek.

Charles stepped into the kitchen, dragging his boy slippers across the floor so slowly that they caught Heidi's attention. "Hi," he said quietly to Bridget. What to do with a babysitter. "What's Jackie doing tonight?" he asked.

"A model," Bridget answered. "Have any model cars I can help you with, Charles?"

"Nah," he replied to the floor. "I'll be downstairs," he told his mom.

"Charlotte?" Bridget called, looking about. Charlotte was in her room on the floor, playing jacks and dealing with tears. She didn't like the idea of her mom going away to a meeting.

"Charlotte?" Jessie also called. "Excuse me," she said to Bridget, then walked down the hallway to her daughter's room. She saw the worried look in Charlotte's eyes. "I won't be long," Jessie told her. "Bridget's here. I see she brought a new book to read."

"Lucy doesn't like her," Charlotte said as her kitten stretched on the pet blanket beside her.

Jessie took Charlotte by the hand and gently led her out to the kitchen and dinette. Bridget smiled at Charlotte and said, "I have some new blush makeup, and if it's okay with your mom, maybe we could dress up a little before your mom gets home." She looked at Jessie. "Would that be okay?"

Charlotte looked up at her mom with easier eyes as her mom smiled and nodded just as Charles burst back upstairs and into the kitchen.

"Can we play Snap?" he said.

"No!" Charlotte yelled. "We're doin' something else!"

Charles was shuffling cards. Jessie said to Bridget, "If you find that Jackie would like to come over for a half hour or so to play cards with Charles, that would be okay. It's up to you."

Jessie gathered her purse and placed her spiral stenographer's notepad inside with two pencils and a pen. "I should be home by nine thirty or so, I guess. I'll be at the school," she repeated to Bridget. Then, with a wink and hug to Charlotte, Jessie stepped into the garage, lifted the garage door, and backed the little Corvair out of its space. She stepped out to close the garage door again, then drove down Midville Road to Main Street, picked up her father, a member of the school board, and drove to the high school.

Patricia Ingalls met Jessie there, as Martin McMillan had promised, and she sat with Jessie throughout the meeting. At seven o'clock, roll was called before the open caucus, when the board members, treasurer, and superintendent reviewed the items to be presented at the public meeting at eight. Jessie's pencil began to scribble across the first page of her new notebook. Plans for a presentation at the October PTA meeting would include the discussion of a 2.6-mill renewal and a 4.4-mill operating levy to be on the November ballot. Dr. Cromwell and superintendent Mike Edwards would urge approval of the two tax measures. They would present the fact that school enrollment had doubled in the past ten years while state aid had dropped, and the district would receive some $17,000 less.

The voices sailed up and over, floating down and around, and Jessie felt dizzy as her tablet pages filled quickly with new lingo, and she scribbled and pushed her pencil forward. She held her breath without thinking about it and found her hand stiff in strain. Finally the talk paused. *Remember to breathe.* She glanced up at the faces around her. The lights were so bright.

"There's always more agenda at the August meeting," Patricia Ingalls whispered, tapping Jessie's arm gently.

At eight o'clock the official meeting convened; a few more people were permitted into the room and took seats aligning the walls. Mr. Edwards brought the meeting to order and asked everyone to stand for the Pledge of Allegiance. Next were the roll call and a moment of silence for an elder, retired board member who had just passed away. Approval of the previous meeting minutes ... financial statements ... bills paid ... milk bids. The milk contract was awarded to Hewes Dairy. Jessie scribbled hastily; Ingalls nodded to her in approval. A new bus was purchased, and a driver was hired.

"We have two new family members," the superintendent broke in. "Jessie," he said, and she raised her head to find everyone looking at her. "Jessie Conrad will be taking the place of Patricia Ingalls for the *Post* since Patricia is moving to an editorial desk at the paper. Welcome, Jessie." Mr. Edwards smiled.

Jessie raised her pencil, which was shaking, and smiled at the room with a timid "Thank you" as the group, including her father, applauded lightly.

Mr. Edwards continued, "We also are excited to introduce Terrence Warne, our new basketball coach." Mr. Warne stood tall at his chair and gave a slight bow. "Mr. Warne is a graduate of Ohio University, where he played ball, and we expect him to pool our talent together"—the superintendent thrust his fist into the air—"into a great season." The assembled group again clapped their hello.

The next morning Jessie rose at six o'clock, made a cup of instant coffee under the ceiling light of her little kitchen, and took a sip, looking out the sink window at the sunrise just beginning to light the horizon to the east over the Bauer farm. She had enjoyed the meeting, but her sleep had been restless.

She went to their kitchen table with her tablet and meeting notes, and looked at them, flipping through the pages in thought. Her pencil began to move across the fresh paper to begin composing a report according to the samples she had studied. She wrote the header, the date, and her opening sentence: "The Clover Township School Board met Tuesday evening in West Emmette to discuss agendas for the new school year." For some reason she felt comfortable. She created paragraphs of the topics discussed, hoping the newspaper editor would smooth them out this first time.

Her telephone bell rang with the first call of the day. Jessie stepped to the phone quickly. The children were still asleep. It was Patricia Ingalls, calling to see whether she had any questions. *How kind*, Jessie thought as she ended the call. It was now seven o'clock. She needed to call the paper's city desk number at seven-thirty. Her palms began to perspire. She looked over her notes again, wondering whether she should include the exact salaries stated.

She thought of the new basketball coach. He would be the last item, she determined. This was exciting news. "Terrence Warne was hired by the board as the new health and physical education teacher and high school varsity basketball coach," she wrote. "Mr. Warne, from Dayton, is a graduate of Ohio University, where he played basketball and earned his bachelor degree in education." Jessie decided to add a quote here. "'We welcome Mr. Warne and his wife, Judy, and their two young sons and trust they will enjoy our student and parent enthusiasm for the sport,' Mr. Edwards said."

Jessie set her now-dulled pencil down, read over her report, and went back to the phone to call the city desk at the number Martin had noted. A woman there took Jessie's dictation and said she would give the report to Martin. Jessie hung up the black phone receiver in tremendous relief, and with an audible exhale, she clasped the handle for a few moments, looking at the phone and her empty coffee cup.

Just then Charles walked out to the kitchen in his pajamas and sat down at the table. He was tugging at his sock and pulling it away from his right ankle.

"What is it?" Jessie asked.

"Just an itch."

"Let me take a look," his mom said. She knelt down to check her son's skin. "Well, it isn't an insect bite. Looks like a rash. We'll see."

But that night, Charles's rash was worse. It was redder, and some bubbles had formed in the middle. And now there was a new patch of it forming on Charles's left ankle.

"Looks like poison ivy," Jessie said nervously, and she led Charles to the bathroom cupboard. "Here, sit on the edge of the tub." She opened the small cabinet near the bathroom door, which held all the family medicine: ointments, aspirin, bandages, iodine, camphor, and sweet oil. "We'll put on some calamine lotion."

The itch was terrible now. Charles had dug at it all day, and his socks had made it worse. Jessie dabbed the pink liquid onto the rash with a cotton ball, and it began to dry over the red skin. The topical medicine felt good but didn't mask the itch very well.

"This will help the rash to dry up. You need to try to not itch it, if you can," she instructed sympathetically. "There." She put the bottle top back on. "You can get ready for bed, and let's have some popcorn."

Jessie went to the kitchen sink and turned on the faucet. When the water reached her hands, she felt a flashback, a vivid memory of Matthew's skin, sunburned from working on the house outside in the summer, his skin shedding in great peels.

The next morning, before Charles and Charlotte woke up, Jessie pulled out from the antique washstand cabinet the heavy medical book her father had given her. The book was four inches thick in a taped-up, deep-green cover with the faded title *The Practical Home Physician*. It was dated 1911, but her dad had said that every medical answer was inside. She flipped the two-pound volume to its back pages and index, and she looked up "poison ivy." She found "Poison Ivy, Poison Oak, Poison Sumac" listed on pages 450 and 451. She turned to page 450. There she read of several applications; one was "Borax—Two drachms; Glycerin—Two ounces; Water—Two ounces." Another called for half a drachm of camphor, one ounce of oxide of zinc, and one ounce of starch, "this is to be dusted thickly upon the skin." The next paragraph was about freckles, and she wished she were dealing with freckles instead of poison ivy.

The powder application didn't help, so Jessie took Charles to Dr. Cromwell's office the next afternoon. Charlotte of course had to go along. Dr. Cromwell's office was built into the front of a large 1900 redbrick home on Main Street. He had cleared the side lot for the parking of a few cars, creating a gravel space to the right. Charlotte and Charles were deathly quiet in their walk up the wooden porch steps with their mom. On the large open porch, which still had a swing, Jessie pulled a screen door outward, then pushed a loudly creaking oak door inward. She wondered how much this visit would cost.

As the three Conrads sat in the smooth, heavy captain's oak chairs on the wood-planked floor in the waiting room, which thirty-five years before had been Judge Foust's dining room, afternoon light filtered in through the white window blinds. They heard some boys' voices amplify and then fade from the sidewalk as their bikes passed Dr. Cromwell's front porch.

"The guys are going to the ball field," Charles told his mom. Jessie wondered again how much this visit would cost.

Dr. Cromwell's nurse called Charles's name, and all three stood together and followed Mrs. Scott into a narrow hallway. The wood-paneled floor creaked below their cautious steps. The smell of alcohol and medicine rose and punched their noses. The nurse led them to a room and told Charles to step up and sit on a table, where some white paper was draped over the side. A stool was there.

Jessie held Charlotte on her lap in a chair to the side of the small exam room, and there they waited for Dr. Cromwell. Jessie said quietly to Charles, "Would you mind if I ask Dr. Cromwell, while we're here, about the nosebleeds you've been having?"

"No," Charles replied with lowered head. His sudden nosebleeds had sent him out of the classroom on several occasions at school. The three Conrads heard Dr. Cromwell's voice saying goodbye to a Mr. Cooke, a patient who was leaving another room. There was a very still pause, and then their door, which had been left slightly ajar, pushed slowly open.

Dr. Cromwell heavily entered. He was a tall man with black hair and big, bushy eyebrows. He actually wasn't bad looking, except for those thick eyeglasses; Charles and Charlotte's heads turned upward to see the tall, towering man in a white coat with a dimpled, hair-stubbed chin. He had the eyes of a raccoon with broom-like eyelashes. And he had a clipboard.

"Hi, Jessie," he said in a deep, husky voice. "It was nice to see you again—at the board meeting. Interesting session, huh?" And then he turned to Charles. "And you, young man, what have you done?" Charles raised his pant leg to reveal the blistered skin.

"Wow!" Dr. Cromwell said, looking at Charles's raging rash and swollen ankles. "Yes, that's a poison ivy rash. You are going to need an antibiotic to clear that!" He wrote a prescription on a tablet of paper but then said to Jessie, "I think we have some samples in the closet. He should start them tonight. I'll write the directions."

Then he turned again to Charles. "Do you know how to make a pack of oatmeal?" Charles nodded, though he didn't. "Smear some on your rash and try to sit still with it for a half hour at a time to calm the itch. No socks.

"Let's see," he continued, looking into the new family file. "I have no records forwarded yet." Dr. Cromwell glanced at Charlotte. "Hi, Charlotte," he said with a smile. Then he turned back to Jessie. "How are we on immunizations? Did the children receive their polio vaccine in Columbus?"

"Yes," Jessie answered. "Remarkable, isn't it?"

"We had an assembly at school and dispensed the vaccine here last year,"

Dr. Cromwell said. "I read that next year a liquid form might be available."

The nosebleeds were discussed, and after a brief examination, Dr. Cromwell said that such nosebleeds were often caused by stress and asked that they monitor occasions for a few more weeks. He smiled at Charles, shook his hand, and said, "I don't see anything physically to worry about, son. Keep a handkerchief handy. Blow your nose gently for a while." Then to Jessie he said, "Be sure to have your medical records forwarded to us from Columbus soon. We need to follow up on any additional immunizations." Then he said goodbye and left the room.

Meadow Drive seemed like miles away. The children moved quietly in a sort of numb aftershock to the waiting room chairs, while Jessie checked with Dr. Cromwell's secretary at the counter. She told Jessie that the cost of today's visit would be three dollars. Jessie opened her wallet, handed the money to the girl with a thankful smile, took the packet of antibiotics, and, most relieved and grateful, ushered her children in hand back to their beige Corvair.

That evening Jessie set up their family card table in the center of the living room and began to teach Charles and Charlotte how to play Five Hundred, which they would practice and practice over the next five days while Charles's blisters dried up. Their copy of yesterday's newspaper lay open on the kitchen table to the "Local" section and the page with Jessie's first article in print. There was no byline yet, no credit, but that was okay. *Maybe down the road*, Jessie thought.

CHAPTER 7

It wasn't the letter that moved Jessie to call Emma Wolfe. It was the dream about Walter. Had it been a dream? Or had she just recalled the image of Charles, Charlotte, and Walter approaching the house that day ... that afternoon in October in Columbus when she waited at the front door for her children to come home, when she would tell them the news of their father? She recalled seeing the three children approach, walking home from school. Emma was outside too on their Harmony Street, waiting on her front yard next door to intercept Walter. Emma bid a brief, broken hello to Charles and Charlotte that day, taking Walter by the shoulder and pulling him close to her as they watched the two Conrad children move on to their mother. Walter had watched his best friends from across the yard as his mother explained to him what had happened to Mr. Conrad, while Jessie told her children the same. Walter listened in fear as his little life began to change too.

When Jessie called Emma on the telephone this late August morning, she told her friend in Columbus about Charles's poison ivy and her new job, and Emma told Jessie that no, Walter hadn't found a good friend like Charles yet. Emma thanked Jessie for the birthday card and said again that they all missed the Conrad Three very much, and she desperately wished they could still be neighbors.

The little house at 147 at the top of the street led the pattern of electric life that soon formed a chain down the slope and bend of Meadow Drive. Three more houses were finished and sold, and the street was almost fully occupied by the time the county fair opened.

On Wednesday night at the end of August, the night before Charlotte and Charles would go to the fair for the first time, Jessie packed her two pies in a basket, then helped the children choose what clothes they would wear the next morning.

"We need to get up early," she told them. "I have to be at the church tent by seven thirty." The three were in Charles's room.

Charles pulled a shirt from his drawer. "Is this okay?" It was a striped, short-sleeve, collared polo shirt. And he chose his navy shorts.

"I think so," Jessie said. "It's going to go up to eighty-eight degrees tomorrow, they say. But take your sweatshirt with you because it could be chilly in the morning." That seemed impossible.

In Charlotte's room, Charlotte had set out her new floral T-shirt and some pink pedal pushers. "Good choice," Jessie said, smiling. "You too. Take a sweater too. Your old navy one. You'll get dirty probably." She set the chosen clothing across the foot of their beds.

The heat of late summer along with its humidity had swelled in the house through the day and was locked inside the little ranch by nightfall. The living room smelled like swollen wood and varnish. It was hot. All three bedrooms' double-hung windows were pushed up as high as they could go with the curtains pulled back. There was no breeze tonight.

Charlotte crawled atop her quilt as Jessie turned on the twelve-inch Polar Cub rotating fan, which was set on top of her dresser. Charlotte, dressed in shortie cotton pajamas, lay on top of her sheets, arms flung out to the side as though floating on water. The electric fan began whirring in its alto song, turning its metal head to the left and then to the right. The fan paused at its right pivot stop, then resumed its course. Charlotte waited for its pushed air to pass over her skin. Left. Right. Left. Right. Every twelve long seconds.

A fan ran in Charles's room too. But it wasn't the heat that would keep Charles awake. When his mom bade him good night at the door, Charles said, "I recounted my coins for the fair."

"How much did you save?" Jessie asked.

"Five dollars and thirty-five cents. What should I buy?"

"Whatever you like."

Jessie's alarm clock rang at six the next morning. Dawn was just breaking, the morning birds were talking, and the air had finally cooled. One, two, three—on went the bedroom lights at 147. Charlotte and Charles were dressed within three minutes and at the breakfast table, with their wallets set in wait at their spoons. Charlotte was going to carry a small purse, and in it she packed tissue like her mother and some lip balm.

Jessie, still in her robe, poured some milk and instant chocolate mix into their glasses, and they hurried their breakfasts along. The long-handled teaspoons jingled in the slightly rounded glass tumblers as they each stirred their drinks. Jessie set out some grocery store pastries, then excused herself to get dressed.

The fairgrounds were sixteen miles away. The Conrads drove down Meadow Drive past some other houses with their morning lights on too, where other families were also getting ready for the fair.

They turned left onto Main Street; then after two miles, they turned onto North Township Road. They passed the Morgan farm, which was quite still, for that family was already at the fair for the week, staying with their animals. Mr. Morgan was also a member of the fair board, Jessie remembered. They would pick up Ethel at her house, then go on down North Township Road all the way to Benton. In Ethel's driveway, Ethel jumped in the right front seat of her sister's car with her usual cheery greeting, and as Jessie backed the Corvair back out onto Flag Street, Ethel turned toward Charles and Charlotte and said, "Look what I found in my shoes this morning!" And she handed them each two quarters.

The little Corvair turned again onto Township Road, driving west for another five miles to Lardonbrook Road. Charlotte clutched her purse. Jessie turned the little car to the right at the light, and they moved northwest across the map, up and down a beautiful stretch of road over higher farmland. They went left onto Meadow Creek Road, past the scout camp, and across more dips in the blacktop lane, past some pretty estates and horse farms.

Ahead on the right was a large, open field and a gravel entry marked "Fair Gate 3." The morning air was crisp and fresh, and they could begin to hear some faint noises from the fairgrounds. Charlotte pulled herself forward to peer up over the front car seat, while her mom slowed the car through the entrance drive and onto a grassy lot. Some men were waving flags to tell her where to park. The car ride became much bumpier now that they went across open field, and Charlotte and Charles could barely contain their excitement. Charles had rolled down his window and moved his hand to the car door handle as they entered a space on the grass next to another car, whose family had parked and was stepping out.

"Wait, Charles," Jessie said. "Wait to open the door until the car stops."

The car finally settled on a grassy knoll, the engine was turned off, and Charles and Charlotte jumped out. Jessie and Ethel grabbed their straw hats and pie baskets, and as the four began to walk across the field to the ticket gate, they heard a tinny, wondrous sound in the distance. As they walked toward it, Jessie asked Charles to stay close to Charlotte all day. He was already holding her hand.

"All day?" Charles said.

"Yes. Come with me to the church tent, and after I get started, we'll talk about where you can venture to this first morning."

As the four approached the fairgrounds, a scene of tents, colors, smoke, grilling, hay, stalls, flags, and strange buildings appeared. The sounds grew louder and louder—of voices over loudspeakers and music and horses neighing. They reached some fencing and met four men with aprons at the entrance, who were collecting tickets. Then Charlotte and Charles entered a paved pathway their mother called a "midway," and into this gloriously happy, new, noisy world they walked, joining the hundreds of other neighbors of Perch County.

Mrs. Douglas and Mrs. Fowler were already at work in the church tent's kitchen when the group reached a large tent with the banner "Old Clover Reformed Church," and inside, the griddles sizzled viciously as large chunks of butter were dropped onto them. Mrs. Douglas asked Jessie to mix the pancake batter and directed Ethel to peel and cut potatoes. Charles and Charlotte sat at one of the six tables on the side, waiting for instructions. Charlotte's head turned left as she watched some young women walk by with four small, obedient billy goats, and she saw some men pushing carts of supplies. She noticed a few girls in straw cowgirl hats. Charles's head was turned in the other direction; he was looking at the rides three midways over.

Jessie soon went to her two children and told them they could leave the tent and walk around for a short time. "Charles, you see where we are. This is Strawberry Lane. The tractors on display are right over there." She pointed to a nearby corner of grass, where numerous red and green tractors were lined up. "Hold Charlotte's hand and stay within these first two or three midway lanes or just make a circle. Then come back here and check in … in, well, twenty minutes this first time."

Charles looked at his watch, his dad's watch, which still was large on his young, pale wrist. It was nine o'clock. The brother and sister left and returned in exactly twenty minutes, and the next time Jessie gave them a half hour. "Be back here at ten o'clock. I'll be able to leave with you to go on rides at noon."

This time Charlotte pulled her brother to the souvenir stand she had noticed on their first walk. It was a large trailer cart draped with silver necklaces and bracelets that hung from roof-lined rods like icicles on a Christmas tree. The bright morning air tossed the jewelry slightly to and fro in a teasing sort of sparkle. But it was the figurines in the case below that drew Charlotte's attention. There, three rows deep, were figurines of cats; and Charlotte, still holding Charles's hand, leaned down closely to the glass case. "Look, CJ! See that one?" She pointed to a small tan-colored figurine of a kitten sitting in a sweet pose, with two plastic whiskers striking out from the world's cutest nose. "That's the one I want!"

Charles looked up at the man behind the counter, who had stepped over to the young customers. "Can I help you?" the man said. He was dark haired, had a mustache, and looked a little like Mr. Howards at church.

Charles asked him, "How much is that kitten … there?" He pointed. Charlotte's eyes were glued to her prize, and her breath quickened as the man reached into the case to withdraw the figurine.

"One dollar," he answered.

Charles leaned down to Charlotte, who eagerly opened her purse and reached down into the sacred bag for her change purse. "That's four quarters," he whispered to his sister. "Do you have them?"

Just then Jackie Walker ran up behind the two. "Charles!" he yelled, slapping his neighbor on the back. "What are you doing here?"

Charlotte poured her change into her small cupped hand. Two dimes fell into the grass below. Charles stooped down and retrieved them. "Here, put your money in my hands and count out four quarters." She did so while the man in the booth prepared a paper bag for the little kitten figurine; he pulled from the figurine a small price sticker, which read "two dollars," and wrapped it in a small piece of tissue paper.

Jackie had pulled Charles aside to show him the baseball cards he bought, and after Charlotte gave the man her coins with a shy "Thank you" and great excitement in her little chest, she took the small, brown bag and, clutching it with both hands and her purse, she turned and bumped into some tall legs walking past her. Suddenly she was fenced in behind passing groups of men and women and strollers, and she couldn't see Charles. In a panic, she looked left and right in the filtered, bright August sun, and stepped out onto the busy walkway. The noise of voices and music and tractors seemed loud. She looked up at the strange faces and felt a surge of fear and tears building when suddenly Charles grabbed her hand. Charlotte struggled to reclasp her bag and purse with the other hand.

"C'mon!" Charles called. "Jackie wants us to see this baseball card stand." And Charles pulled his little sister into the crowd, and the two walked fast behind their friend.

But Charles didn't pay attention to the direction they were walking, and after Jackie said goodbye, Charles looked around. More people were moving happily hither and yon, more people than earlier in the morning. The sounds were louder too. Charles held Charlotte's hand so tightly that she said, "Ow!" and tried to pull it loose.

"Where do we go?" Charlotte asked.

"I'm not sure." Charles didn't see the tractor lawn, and this midway sign said "Apple Lane." "Let's walk this way a little."

And the two went farther and farther from the church tent. Soon they came to an open building with some big pigs, and there was a building beside that, with a wide doorway and some calling out inside—someone talking on a microphone. The brother and sister peered inside to see some cattle being led forward one by one onto a dirt arena. A man in overalls came up behind them, gently took Charles's shoulder to step him aside, and said, "Excuse me" as he tried to enter. Charles looked up and saw that the man wore a farmer's cap.

Charles led Charlotte back outside and looked about. There was a booth across the way marked "Information," and Charles led Charlotte over to it. Then he spoke to the woman inside.

"I think we're lost," he said. Charles heard Charlotte gasp.

The woman said to Charles, "Don't worry, son. Are your parents on the fairgrounds?"

"Yes, my mom is working at our church tent."

"Go over there by the grandstand near that window there." She pointed at a very large building across a wide-open lawn with benches and a few trees. "See?" she said. "See the lost-and-found window? The man inside will call out your names, and your mom should hear. She'll come to get you. If she doesn't hear and you're still waiting, come back over here to me, and we'll walk together to your mom's booth."

Ten very long minutes later, Jessie was at the grandstand lost-and-found window, scooping Charlotte up in her arms and patting Charles on the shoulder. She had her purse with her and, catching her breath, said, "I'm sorry, I'm sorry. We'll do better tomorrow. Charles, you did the right thing. Let's go have some fun." And with an iron smile and glistening eyes, Jessie led her two lambs off toward the rides, while the woman in the information booth across the lawn also watched them with glistening eyes.

That night Charlotte placed the precious knickknack up on her dresser top beside the framed photo of herself in the ballerina tutu, where the little porcelain kitten would sit overlooking her bed and bedroom and dreams.

As Charlotte fell contently into a deep, carefree sleep, her Grandfather Hall was repairing a newly acquired clock, holding in hand the inner intricate gears and works of a Gilbert porcelain shelf clock. He drew slow puffs of licorice tobacco from his brier pipe. He set down the delicate cluster of parts to log the clock's progress, then wiped its scrolled, ornate porcelain frame with a cotton cloth until he heard the drop of some keys outside. He glanced over at the Rupp rifle, with its narrow wrist and unusual architecture, its beautiful inlay and charred oil finish. Then he went to the front room, which wasn't lit, and looked out the window at a quiet, dark sidewalk. It appeared to be still.

The fair ended on Labor Day night, and on the next day, a Tuesday, while the farmers were moving the pigs and sheep and goats back to their farms, and while the tractors were being driven onto trailer ramps and others driven down the road, and while the prize-winning quilts were brought carefully down one at a time, and while the flower arrangements were collected for use on various church altars and the apple and pepper displays were packed for donation, Jessie set out the clothes her children would wear tomorrow for their first day of second and fourth grades. The house was quiet. Charles was off somewhere with Mitch and Bobby—probably in the woods; and Charlotte had taken her new kitten knickknack down to Becky's house.

In Charles's room, Jessie brought out the new twill pants and short-sleeved plaid shirt they had bought at Sears last week. She had pressed both. She hoped Matthew would have approved were he with them. The shoes ... what shoes? She went to the closet and pulled out his Sunday brown tie shoes. She would ask Charles to polish them when he got home and make sure they still fit. She had fifty-seven dollars in the checking account, and the next check from Social Security would come on September 9. She hoped the shoes still fit.

When Jessie entered Charlotte's room, she glanced around, stepping over some crayons and a coloring book. She picked up a book from the rug and placed it back in the book box beside the little rocker. She looked at the rocker Matthew had carved and fashioned for his young daughter, noticing for the first time that Charlotte had outgrown the small seat. She would need to put it away soon in the basement or the attic.

Jessie slid open the closet door to reach for the new dress they had also bought last week, but she noticed an odd, somewhat sour smell. Jessie looked about the floor of the closet, pushed aside Charlotte's weathered black tie shoes and some shoeboxes with clippings of comics and leaves from the yard. There was the Terri Lee doll trunk and rocks; then ... there, in the far back corner, was a notecard box she didn't recall giving to Charlotte. She pulled it out and opened the lid to find ... a dead bird. A small, dead, young ... robin, maybe.

Jessie pushed the bedroom window farther up to let more air into the room and carried the box out to the garage; she took a shovel and the box to the woods and buried the little bird. She marked the small mound of earth with a Popsicle stick. Smiling, she returned to the kitchen and washed her hands, went back to the bedroom, wiped the floor down, then pulled out the dress for tomorrow. She liked the dress. It was plaid, the new blue and red plaid, with a white collar. Charlotte would also need to wear her church shoes tomorrow; then she could wear her favorite black lace ones Thursday. They were so scuffed now, she thought, looking them over, but soon she would outgrow them.

The next morning at 6:45, the school routine resumed. Jessie met Charles and Charlotte in the kitchen and set the cereal boxes on the breakfast table. She served the orange juice she had mixed the night before as the cereals poured forth into each bowl again. Milk, bakery roll. By 7:20 they were in their little Corvair and off to Main Street below, where Jessie would park the car, put on her crossing guard hat and belt, and hold the sign aloft in the middle of the street until her first two schoolchildren, her own, were safely across the quiet street and to the school sidewalk.

Once again, Mr. Powell stepped outside to greet them. He shook Charles's hand and then gave a slight bow to Charlotte as they walked past him and went into the building. Then he walked out to greet Jessie. "Thank you again for continuing on the job, Jessie. Any questions?"

"No, Robert. Thank you. I appreciate the job."

"We're glad to have you, and we thank you." Mr. Powell crossed the street with Jessie, where she waited for the approaching children.

"Are you ready for a new school year?" Jessie said politely.

"Yes, indeed!" Mr. Powell replied, clasping his hands behind his back and clicking his heels. He waited as five children arrived at the crosswalk, and he walked back across with them as Jessie held up her sign in the middle of the street. All the children returning to school this first week of September had a red-orange brightness to their faces—suntanned from being at the fair. Jessie, with the final two children crossing late for school at one minute past eight, stepped back to let two cars move on through Main Street and heard the first school bell ring.

Her father watched from his parlor window. There was his young daughter, widowed already and nearly as tragically as he had been widowed with the loss of his own wife and Jessie's mother, so young. Jessie would need to share the beauty of the earth with her children in a different way now, he thought, telling her mentally that there was a whole energy beyond what we could see. "No one else's experience will compare to yours or ease your pain," he whispered aloud to her through the windowpane. "Your sadness is singular, your own. Embrace it," he whispered knowingly, "as if a blessing, and wear it like a scar. Or a sweater," he added, changing the metaphor.

"Class! We are going to have a very exciting year!" Mrs. Shore called out in front of her new gathering of second grade pupils. In the back of the room near the coat rack, lunch boxes lined the shelves, but coats and hats weren't yet needed, and the row of silver hooks remained empty in wait. "This year we will study language, handwriting, and history. And in music class, I will teach you how to square-dance!"

Charlotte's heart leaped with excitement, and so did Susan's, and the two girls looked at each other with joy. Stevie slunk down into the wooden seat, sliding a bit under his desk, while Sebastian, seated in the back row and wearing a tie and church shirt, was drawing Charlotte's name in his notebook over and over.

"After lunch we will move into our assigned seats alphabetically," Mrs. Shore added, beginning her first lesson plan for the year.

Back home, Jessie set her stop sign and deputy hat down on the garage shelf, where they would rest until she would return to school for afternoon dismissal duty at three o'clock. As she approached the back door step leading up into the kitchen, she noticed a folded paper tucked into the storm door handle. Heidi barked from inside in nervous warning through the door. Jessie unfolded the half piece of notebook paper, which was smudged a bit with dirt, and read it. Poorly scribbled in pencil, the note said,

> Ask your daddy who the TRUE owner of the
> Rupp rifle is.

Jessie looked about, wondering what this meant, saw no one, and carried the mysterious note inside, where she was greeted by their little off-white dog who was extra eager to welcome her home. Jessie swooped up her precious puppy for comfort, gave her a hug, and tucked the disturbing note into the phone stand. She didn't notice that the spare key to her father's house had been removed from the garage shelf.

It was Wednesday, and Jessie was a day behind in chores because of the fair. The laundry and ironing would both need to be done today.

Jessie carried the dog with her to the bathroom closet to get the wicker laundry hamper. She paused to slide out the weight scale, kept on the floor next to the hamper, and stepped on it, holding her pet. It said 117 pounds. "Perfect," she said, fluffing the hair on Heidi's head, and she lovingly set the little dog back down on the floor. "You weigh twelve pounds, Heidi."

Jessie pulled the towels from their posts and carried the laundry hamper to the basement. She put the first load in the washing machine and, returning upstairs, decided to skip the bed sheets for one week. She went to the kitchen to get the notebook she had purchased for newspaper work. She looked at the wall above the telephone stand and thought it would be a nice spot for the violets painting, looking at the bare, painted plaster and imagining it there. She would enjoy seeing it again.

Opening the notebook and taking a pencil, she scribbled some hovering thoughts about something Charlotte had fun doing this summer—making a make-believe soup from weeds. When Jessie would send Charlotte outside to dig up dandelions in their new lawn, Charlotte would kneel here and there with her little trowel and plastic pail, but then she was soon distracted to gather other weeds—ragweed, English plantain caps, chicory, Queen Anne's lace—and would come back with this make-believe "soup."

This she shared with Ethel when her sister walked in the back door just then. "Then Charlotte mixes it all with the milk from milkweed pods from the farm lane, along with the pod scales and silk."

Ethel smiled. "What? Are you writing an article?"

"No. No, I was thinking of a children's story or something. I was just getting started. I don't know."

"Like a picture book?"

"Yeah, I guess so. I can't draw, but I thought I would try to make a little story."

"What do you have so far?" Ethel urged.

Jessie looked down at her spiral steno book. "Just ... 'Hi! My name is Charlotte!'" Jessie looked up at her sister.

"Well, okay, that's a good start," she said. And the two sisters broke into laughter, as did perhaps the plastic ducks outside. Heidi paced a few circles near Jessie's white tennis shoes in the happy commotion.

"How did the kids do, going back to school?" Ethel asked.

"Just fine. They were excited actually."

"Did you see Daddy this week yet?" Ethel asked.

"No, why?"

"He seems a little tired, is all."

"Well." Jessie paused. "That's not like Daddy."

"I know."

"Maybe I'll stop in this afternoon before crossing duty."

"How was that job again this morning?" Ethel asked, her eyes in sparkle.

"Good. Fine. It does help," Jessie answered. "It's kinda fun even." She paused. "I've had a letter from Matthew's Aunt Myrtle." She walked over to the telephone stand and reached for the envelope. "She sent some cash," Jessie added with gratitude, showing her sister the letter. Ethel read Myrtle's words. "Perry and I sure wish you could come down to see us. We sure would like to see the children. Things would have to change a lot before we can make a trip north again."

"Is she referring to your Uncle Perry's arthritis?" Ethel asked.

"Yes," Jessie said, taking back the pages. "Obviously we can't afford to go to Florida. I miss them." In the backyard, crows were arriving one by one again, lighting down like black parachutes to eat the additional grass seed Jessie had dispersed onto some bare spots. Robins stayed on the yard closer to the house, finding worms near the summer petunias, which were still blooming along the foundation block.

Jessie placed the letter back in the telephone stand and paused, deciding to show Ethel the strange message she had found in the back door. She pulled the rumpled slip of paper out from under the phone book. "Ethel, I found this note tucked in my back door this morning when I came home from crossing duty." She handed the piece of paper to Ethel, whose expression dropped in concern.

"What could this mean?" Ethel said, annoyed by the mysterious note.

"I don't know," Jessie replied. "I'll ask Daddy, sometime. Maybe. I don't know."

Ethel picked up her car keys. "What's today? Wednesday. We'll ask Daddy on Saturday. Yes, we need to ask. I guess we can wait to ask Saturday. I'll ask Jacob what he thinks." She swung her white purse into position. "Frances said she's coming to town Saturday. She wants to take us all to the dairy. Especially Charlotte and Charles."

"Oh, that's nice. I guess Saturday will be okay," Jessie said as Ethel left.

Charles, at school during his first day of fourth grade, was hungry and happy when the eleven o'clock lunch hour arrived. He carried his lunch box into the cafeteria hall behind Jackie and Bobby, who paused to buy a chocolate milk bottle just inside the door. Charles's lunch box had a thermos filled with an orange drink. The boys settled in at one of the long tables at the end of the bright room, whose large windows ran the length of the lunchroom and looked out on the playground. Charles eagerly ate his bologna sandwich, carrot sticks, and chips; and he peeled the hard-boiled egg, while his friends swapped sandwiches. The boys talked about their new teacher and shared fair experiences while Charles's eyes followed the custodian, carrying a bucket in quiet mission and shuffle, his keys dangling from his belt; a large toolbox swung from his left hand like a counterweight. The man whistled quietly under his cap as he passed behind the boys and tables, and exited the room. Charles saw him enter a doorway out in the hall, his head disappearing downward into a shadow, obviously going down some steps.

The first three days of school passed, and the following sultry September Saturday brought Frances. Frances was Ethel and Jessie's older cousin, a tall, lanky spinster from Pittsburgh, who often wore men's pinstriped suits and spoke in a trumpet kind of voice—high and lively. She had pepper-gray hair, and her age was irrelevant. Every so often she appeared in town, driving her big red '59 Cadillac DeVille, cigarette posted out the window. Frances had sent one of the more thoughtful letters to Jessie after Matthew's accident, telling Jessie to stretch her imagination and also to read a book about after-death experiences. Had she heard of Richard Feynman? Frances asked. Frances also expressed a sentiment, as the letter went on, wondering whether she too should have married and had children, saying how blessed she thought Jessie was to be a mother.

On this Saturday Frances pulled into the driveway at 147, tooted her Cadillac horn, and Jessie, Charles, and Charlotte closed the house and rushed outside to greet her. "Get in!" the woman crowed above her big jaw. "Henry's not coming because he's preparing to take some of his clocks to a show in Canton." Bird, Ada, and Ethel were in the car. The three Conrads squeezed in.

Frances was a dairy chemist, a scientist when women in the field of agriculture were few. Her car windows were open; she drove one-handed with her right hand on the wheel, her tall back leaning toward the left as she pointed her cigarette high in dramatic fashion. Her head and voice tilted up with natural interest and confidence, and Charlotte was never sure—in her back seat by the fancy door handle—how safe to feel. Frances boomed, "So what kind of ice cream are you going to get today, Charles?"

They were already arriving at the Hewes Dairy, a small block building at the wide bend of Route 270. Beyond that point, there were all farms. Inside the dairy, Frances hailed all the workers by name. Each member of the Conrad family was given a custard cone; then they followed Frances to an office for something she needed. Soon they filed back into the Cadillac.

"Did you see the excavation going on down Midville Road?" Frances called out to her passengers as they reached town again. "Let's drive by," she said eagerly, and the long car turned back onto Midville Road from 270. "I hear that Bill is building a swim lake!"

Frances drove past the Bauer farm and up to the top of the hill, where Meadow Drive began. At the stop sign, where Frances paused ever too briefly—not really coming to a complete stop but letting the big chrome bumper wink at the intersection— Charlotte glanced over at their house in passing. In the short distance, she saw her bedroom window and wished she were in her closet. Frances accelerated, and they sped down past Spade Road, then abruptly slowed to turn left into the lake property drive, Bill Watters's driveway, now a muddy, dusty lane. A truck was parked on the property midway back.

Jessie was embarrassed to be sitting there. She knew about the project. It was a good idea. West Emmette was growing in leaps and bounds as the Zimmers continued to build homes in a greatly whipped flurry.

At the farmhouse across the street, Bill's brother-in-law and sister were sitting on their front porch, rocking in wooden chairs, and talking over naming ideas for the lake. "Look," they said. "There's another looker."

In the front seat, Frances, Ada, and Bird gazed at the mounds of dirt and rocks on the property and at a gaping hole in the ground. Water would be channeled to the pit from the abandoned mine in the back. At the front end of the property, at the road to the left of the gravel entrance, was a running fresh stream, a tributary from the Perch River, their other fresh source of water, which ran under the road to another small fishing lake across the street. It guaranteed them a good, clean supply of lake water.

In the distance, across the evolving lake pit, Bill crossed his arms on the tractor, turned off the engine for the day, and watched the great white clouds move across the changing sky. It would soon be time to stop work here for the year and wait for next spring.

While Frances's passengers were looking ahead at the land, Charles's head was turned backward to see who was fishing. There was one boy on the side bank with his pole line in the water. *That would be Timmy Parson*, Charles thought.

Frances put the car in reverse again, backed up, and then turned the car in a circle; they left the property and drove back up Midville Road but still did not turn onto Meadow. Instead they drove on to Main Street to take Bird and Ada home.

"Oh! Ruby's here!" Frances exclaimed to Bird. "Too bad we missed her! She could have come along."

How? Jessie thought. *There are already seven in the car.*

Charlotte liked Ruby. Ruby was Bird's sister. She was a schoolteacher somewhere and lived in an attic apartment somewhere. She had a different look, and she lived on a top floor with gabled windows and lace curtains. It was as though she weren't from there. She dressed in lavender or yellow pastel dresses of different fabrics. She had frilled pillows and good blue suitcases, which were always out for some reason.

Her pink-painted smile was pure and deep, and whenever she leaned down to speak to Charlotte, she locked Charlotte's little soul with her deep-set eyes like a shimmery hook. *I've got you,* they seemed to say. Her gaze was comfortable and accepting, with a future in it. It was simple and welcoming, even bewitching. She smelled of lavender, and her hair was … her hair was … white? Silver? Tied up in a pretty twist under a fancy, blue felt hat or diamond clip.

"How was school?" Ruby asked Charles.

"Fine," Charles replied politely. "I get school store duty next week."

Charlotte's face faded from wonder into jealousy. She couldn't wait to be in fourth grade to have her turn in the school store.

The group moved into the house. Charles ran to his grandfather's study to see what he was doing. Charlotte stood by her mother and Aunt Ethel in the kitchen she hated. Aunt Ada set about making some coffee drink concoction with bottled dark, black liquid, and coconut milk. She reached for the end of

Charlotte's ice cream cone and threw it in the waste can before Charlotte could finish it. The dog Chimney came up behind her and licked her fingers. Ada said to Jessie and Ethel, "Those men came by again last night to talk to your dad. I think they are involved in the—you know—the KK something."

Henry called out to his daughter from the other room. "Jessie! Can Charles spend the night?"

Jessie paused with Ada to ask her, "What men? What did Daddy say?"

"He turned them away. It scares me."

Jessie left the kitchen to find her father. The photograph of her mother holding infant Jessie, who was wearing a starched white dress that had the flounce of a bell, hung on the wall to the right of the rare Allan Fowlds grandfather clock in the front parlor. The frame hung on the dark floral wallpaper in the shadow of the clock near the lace-draped mantle. Jessie passed by it quietly again on her way to her father's desk, noticing in this glance that her infant legs in white stockings looked like a bell's clapper. At her father's desk, Charles was looking at his grandfather's balance-wheel invention, a hollow stainless-steel globe on a pin and axel, which Charles watched spin around and around. There she also found her father.

"What are you working on now, Daddy?" Jessie said lovingly.

His desk was strewn with notebook paper, scribbled across fully with thick, dark pencil script. His penmanship—artistic in boldly crossed *t*'s and deeply looped *d*'s—was a penmanship of its own song, reflecting an interesting mind. While a scholarship had never been within reach at a university, it had been his regardless, from his soul and books and adventures.

"I'm writing about my last hunting trip with Indian Jim in Canada," Henry answered. "He told me a story about the evolution of the dog."

Jessie looked down at the shuffle of pages. She saw the headers "Mascgama" and "Trees" on two pages and "Beavers" on another. "Another book?" she asked.

"Yes. The dog story would be the last chapter."

"And what's that in your typewriter? It looks like—"

"'Paul Revere's Ride' by Longfellow. Yes, I'm just typing out a copy for Charles. He and I can go over it later." Henry patted his grandson's shoulder as Charles stepped away to chase Chimney.

"Daddy," Jessie began with uncertain softness, "someone left a note in my door, asking this." She handed the curious paper slip to him from her purse.

Henry read the note and recognized the irregular script. His eyes kept to the paper, and he said nothing.

"Well?" Jessie asked, pulling him back.

"Well," Henry said quietly, "this is written by Jace Field, Harvey's son."

Jessie waited. "And what does he mean?"

"I have a gun given to me by Harvey, his dad. You know who that is." Jessie had met the man when he came to visit her father a few times when she was young. Her father adored the man—considered him a legend. He was a rifle and firearms expert, a collector of powder horns, and an accomplished trapper and hunter. "To mark the publication of my first book," Henry continued, "Harvey gave that Kentucky rifle to me, one I had admired. And one I featured in the book. It's one of the earliest and most authentic Kentucky rifles in existence. The architecture of the gun is highly unusual. Awfully special." Henry paused, glancing up at his daughter. "Harvey didn't think to ask his son first, I guess. The son approached me after his father died and wanted the gun back." Henry lowered his head. "I suppose I should give it to him, but it means so much to me."

Jessie listened, rubbing her forearm with her thumb back and forth, back and forth, listening intensely. "I see."

"I don't think Jace should have a gun, Jessie. I think he's a little … wild. Or restless. Maybe a tiny bit slow or something. I don't think Harvey gave his son any guns."

"I see."

"I don't like it that he put a note on your door."

"I'm not worried about that, Daddy."

"Let me think about this, Jess."

Jessie turned to find Charlotte. "Oh, Dad," Jessie said before stepping away, "I also wanted to ask you something. The piano teacher said we should get a metronome. Would you have one we could borrow?"

"I don't know that a metronome is a good idea, Jessie," he answered.

"Why?"

"It's too rigid. Every song has a pulse, to be communicated by the player. You need to be expressive … and a metronome limits thoughts, feelings." Henry looked up into his daughter's eyes. "It's a soulless machine, Jessie," he said, smiling.

"But Daddy, you of all people are a man about time," Jessie teased.

"Trust me, Jessie," Henry said. "You need to be careful. You need to let Charlotte be creative. Maybe Charles could try a metronome but only if he needs to steady an exercise. And only in the beginning. He'll be turned off." He put his pencil down. "But to answer your question, no, I don't have one." He stood, and Jessie took his arm to join the others, talking a little about the upcoming clock show.

Ada had quietly pulled together a delicious dinner of roasted squash and eggplant with garlic and tomatoes, gathered from her garden, and served the sort of roasted stew with dinner rolls baked from the dough she had prepared in the morning. After dinner the women helped Ada clear and wash dishes. Then everyone thanked her and bade her farewell, including Jessie and Charlotte, who paused outside to look up into the ash tree, where the last of the bees had moved back into the trunk for the night.

Henry Hall gathered his thoughts and Charles's hand to lead his grandson back to his study. Ada had turned the television on. In passing, Henry turned off the television set and led Charles to his desk to read Henry Wadsworth Longfellow's poem together. Barely had they begun, however, when the doorbell rang. Ada greeted Vince from next door and Emmette Schiller, who swung his large bass instrument in through the door. Vince was carrying his trumpet. Behind them was Cecil Grisby.

Henry was now seventy-seven but still played the saxophone fairly well. The men set their cases in the entry and moved noisily to the front room with all the clocks. Cecil sat down at the old player piano. Henry handed a tambourine and drumstick to his grandson, and jazz began to drown out the competing rhythms of the Howard Miller and Seth Thomas clocks.

It would be long after Charles's bedtime that the music would stop, the friends would say goodnight, and Henry M. Hall would lead Charles back to his desk and story. "Tomorrow morning I will take you to my excavation site, up Clover Hill," Henry told Charles. "I'll show you how the Indians marked their paths there by training the tree limbs to grow east and west."

"Mom says you don't go to church because nature is your church," Charles said to his grandfather.

"Well, yes, I guess that's right. However, Charles, I say the Lord's Prayer every day. In fact, more often than that. I think it holds the key. The secret."

"What secret?"

"The secret of life and faith." Henry looked at his growing grandson. "I also say an Indian prayer sometimes."

"How does prayer work, do you think?" Charles said.

"Well, I think prayer sort of steers the boat."

Charles's eyes were growing sleepy as his grandfather pulled his Elgin pocket watch forth, and after a quick glance, he loosened it from its gold chain and set it on the desk near Charles. Henry resumed reading the Paul Revere legend to Charles, who had pulled up a chair close to his grandfather, who sat again on his retired mill stool—a well-worn, round leather seat that twirled with ease in a complete circle on top of a heavy brass spindle base above three carved claw feet. Henry read Longfellow's words.

> Meanwhile, his friend, through alley and street,
> Wanders and watches with eager ears,
> Till in the silence around him he hears,
> The muster of men at the barrack door,

It wasn't long, however, before his grandfather's slow, steady voice, itself deeply leathered and comforting and sweetly scented from his pipe, along with the trotting pace of Longfellow's poem, led Charles into a drowsy state. Henry noticed the boy's head start to drop, even when Charles tried to hold his chin up on his hand; his elbow moved to the corner of the desk, then to his knee. Soon Henry pulled the big boy onto his lap to gain a few more minutes of reading. But after five more lines of the lively fable, Charles's head fell upon his grandfather's shoulder, and Henry Hall led his grandson over to the old couch, where Charles would sleep and have the best dream of his life.

Charles got to miss church the next morning while accompanying his grandfather to Clover Hill; then when Henry drove his grandson home to Meadow Drive, Jessie asked her dad to stay for brunch. The house smelled full of the roasting beef, which Jessie had placed in the oven before church and now pulled from the stove; she somehow made gravy and mashed potatoes by one o'clock, and she added them to the table she had set before they left for church. It was a mastered meal and a crafted mirage the children barely noticed.

Charles ate quickly, then asked to be excused. He ran to his room to grab his flashlight but couldn't find it. "Dang!" he said, looking in his top dresser drawer. "I know I set it here." He slammed the drawer shut, said goodbye to his grandpa with a quick pause to shake his hand and look into his eyes, then ran next door to enlist Jackie to ride bikes with him down the road back to the Watters farm, where the fishing pole sighting of the day before across the street remained fresh in his mind. There they located Timmy, at the swim lake property.

Timmy's Uncle Bill was cleaning the bulldozer to store for the winter. He saw the boys coming. "Now you chaps watch yer step, ya hear?" he called. "Lots of bumps and holes and debris on the property, ya know." Timmy and his guests stood there and watched as the old tractor sputtered into gear. Uncle Bill moved it across the land beyond some mounds of dirt toward his house at the back of the property, at the end of the sloping, long driveway at the forest line.

In the two and three years ahead, there would be trees to clear and cut—some to be fashioned into picnic tables and pavilions. As Bill drove to the end of the first summer of work, he wondered whether they could indeed make some money with this venture. He thought about his sister and of Hopewell Lake. Could they do the same? What did they have to lose? *I had better be careful here,* he reminded himself. *I have two sons to raise.* But all he could see was a lake, a volleyball court, towels on some sand, and a diving board; and all he could hear was his new buddy Simon saying, "Bill, we gotta do this."

The heaven's stars, breathing high above Clover Township, invisible in the daylight but watching nonetheless, saw the parcels of earth changing below after many years of the same labels of ownership. The Zimmer brothers were measuring and marking another new street and logging the dates and names of the new property owners in a book in the county courthouse. Signatures by the new residents and stamps on their deeds made it official. The brothers' hammers and saws would not stop for winter. The walls of the new house across the street from the Conrad home had been formed with drywall, and finish carpentry would soon begin. A new address was added two lots down from the Millers. A Mr. Malloy and his family were moving there from Dayton to be the new principal of West Emmette's growing high school. The Malloys had asked the Zimmers for a larger front porch and a two-car garage.

Ashton Frost was leaving City Furnace to establish his own heating and air-conditioning business for the village from his home basement on Ivy Street, and Chuck Coale was opening an insurance business next to Schiller's Garage. Sebastian Bowmaster's father was just finishing the trim on his own home, which he had been building independently for the past six years on the short street cut between Garden Drive and Thistle Street behind the new Catholic church, beyond a grove of locust and willow trees.

The librarian of the bookmobile was happily requesting more books for her shelves, and in her district library bus trailer, she sorted and refilled science, history, and picture books for her youthful customers.

At Old Clover Reformed Church, the council and members decided to purchase the closed, vacant Lutheran church building next door and set about moving its pews into their own tired sanctuary. It was a very big year. They also installed a new gas hot water system, and Reverend Burchard launched a youth group.

Life was in a swirling bloom of surprise in West Emmette in this first year of the new decade. Charlotte sat on her quilt on the grass in her new yard, leaning back on her young arms, her toes barefoot and curling into the soft cotton patches of the old quilt, her head turned upward as it most often would be throughout life, watching three ducks cross overhead in their flight south below a mammoth, billowy cumulus cloud.

On Monday, when the children returned to the routine of school, temperatures dropped into the cooler fall season. From the grade school hallway, at the stairwell where two long, thick mops marked the entry, and where several brooms of different uses and sizes rested on the landing in the corner, Maxwell Shipp, the custodian, silently shuffled to the basement between two wide-set walls painted a thick, pasty cream white over hand-formed bricks. The deep-set concrete stairs were fine, he thought, trod with years of use and chipped with history, scuffed with oil and soot from work boots; the steps were solid, dependable, and comfortable like the old school building itself.

Down Max went into the cool cavern of gentle thunder, where the blue furnace was doing a good job of sending up heat for the children; he moved confidently below the school classrooms, under the low ceiling of anchored copper water lines and an orchestra of pipes and air ducts. The shut-off valve for the steam heat boiler provided a splash of red along with the occasional work bucket and spare classroom chair among the grays and blues. He looked at the blue back-flow preventer and the pressure regulator, and admired their sturdy connections. Beside the sump pump was a great, white washtub with a crank wringer. Past that, in a small connecting storage room, was a workbench he decided he would expand and repair during the coming year. He would also fashion new coatracks for two classrooms this winter. This he noted on the wall chart he had just anchored. *All running smoothly*, he added. He gathered a few light bulbs for the number-six classroom and started back up the stairs. It would be a good autumn of school for the children.

CHAPTER 8

"Not that one, not that one." Charlotte flipped through the chocolate chip cookies in the tin box in the kitchen, looking for the cookie with the most chocolate pieces. She was at home from school with a sore throat and still in her pajamas.

Jessie tied a menthol-treated handkerchief to her daughter's throat for comfort. Charlotte took her cookie to the living room, with Heidi following, and turned on the television, looking for a cartoon. It was Wednesday noon, and all that was on TV was news. The news person was reading a Christmas message from the president. She checked all three channels. All news.

She sat down with Heidi on the floor, where her mom was clearing a space to make room for the new Christmas tree. It was December 13, and the front room was being readied to anchor the holiday season. Jessie had moved a year away from the tragedy, and perhaps this year she would feel a return of more excitement for her children and herself and know a happier Christmas celebration once again.

Following the afternoon school-crossing duty that day and on their way home, Jessie and Charles bought a tree, a Scotch pine, from the volunteer firemen at the single-engine garage on Baseline Road. She and her son drove it home, anchored to the top of the little car. Charlotte watched as they carried the tree in and placed it in the stand Jessie had positioned and prepared. Outside, a large, brown oak leaf floated in a dance over their backyard, traveling up across the lawn from the back woods and swirling through the air, unwilling to settle on the first dusting of snow below.

Charlotte dressed her Terri Lee doll in the formal pastel-blue dress while her mother and brother worked in the front room. Her half-grown kitten batted at the little accessory shoes tucked inside the doll trunk.

"What do you want for Christmas, Charlotte?" her mother asked.

Charlotte said she would like a chalkboard.

Jessie left the tree and went to the hi-fi cabinet, on which sat the framed photograph of Charles and Charlotte with the real Santa from 1958 at Parson's Department Store in Columbus. She reached for Perry Como's holiday record album and placed the large, black vinyl record on the hi-fi playing table, turning the power knob on.

"Oh there's no place like home for the holidays," the song began. The melody lifted up as Como's happy, liltingly smooth, and comforting voice filled the house. Charlotte picked up Terri Lee and held her out in her taffeta dress, barefoot still, and sent the doll twirling around with her in a dance. Jessie got a pan of water for the tree base and sang along, "To face unafraid the plans that we made" as Como slid through "Winter Wonderland."

Charles filled Heidi's bowl with some dog food and set it down by the stove, then returned to the living room and his mom. "When can I set up the train?" he asked.

"Oh yeah!" Charlotte exclaimed.

"It's for me, not you!" Charles said. "Don't you have a piano lesson to practice?"

"I have a sore throat!" Charlotte answered. A children's book of Christmas hymns, a gift from Mary Bauer and inscribed to the children on the inside front page, rested on the piano stand. The illustration of a young girl at a piano on the front cover, in front of a stained glass window, looked somewhat like Charlotte.

Charlotte turned back to her brother. "And don't you have some homework to do?"

"Let's get the train first and then do decorations," Jessie said, still listening to Perry Como's rich voice on the record. He was now singing "Have Yourself a Merry Little Christmas."

The train and Christmas boxes had been placed in the attic, and she and Charles would need to go up and get them. The access panel to the attic of the thousand-square-foot ranch was located in the ceiling of the storage closet between the living room and the kitchen bay, behind the birch door. Inside, the floor of the closet raised into a step; then the back wall sloped upward from there, for behind it was the basement stairwell. So the space was one of down and up—a sort of conflicting, or even timeless, bend of space behind the birch door. Up above, in the ceiling over the sloped wall, was the two-foot-by-four-foot access panel to the attic.

Standing on the white utility stool her husband had made, Jessie pushed up the ceiling plywood panel, tipping it aside. A rush of cold air came down from the attic into the closet and hallway. Her brothers-in-law and Charles had set their holiday boxes up there, across the rafters, after their first Christmas here last January.

Once Jessie popped open the panel, she stepped aside to let Charles shimmy up. Wearing a thick sweatshirt, he reached up from the stool, grabbed the open frame above with his hand, and walked his tennis shoes up the back wall slope until he could pull himself up between two rafters. Then he stiffened his elbows to buoy himself upward into a sitting position in the twenty-degree air.

"Do you see any ghosts?" Charlotte called to him.

"Be careful!" Jessie said. *Would Matthew approve of this?* she wondered. *Yes.*

Charles leaned and reached over to where his uncle had set the train boxes. His mom had labeled them just that and tied them with twine so they could be turned horizontally and lowered like freight between the rafters. Charles leaned down with the first carton, sending it slowly to his mother's extended reach. They did the same with the second train box, the ornament boxes, and the window candles box. Then there was one more carton of Christmas lights.

Charles then lowered himself down, and Jessie guarded his backward steps down the wall slope and onto the stool, then backward onto the house floor. Jessie reached up and slid the ceiling panel back into place, closed the closet door, then anxiously lifted the box lid to her ornaments, the ones she had collected over the years with her husband. Jessie let Charles clip the lights on the tree, reminding him of how his father would do it—clipping each bulb to a branch. Then came the ornaments; the plastic snowman went to an upper front branch. She handed the spinning stars, one each, to Charles and Charlotte to hang over a yellow-tinted light bulb, where the heat would make the foil spinner inside turn. The blue glass ornament with the snow scene was next. Then came the red glass bell. Charlotte set the twelve-inch green brush trees with attached red glass bulbs, decorative pieces sprayed with a white snow, onto each side of the piano top.

The photograph taken in this living room of the family's 1961 Christmas morning—of Charles holding a new sleeping bag with his right arm and hugging Heidi with his left, and of Charlotte sitting on the floor next to them in her fuzzy, blue-ribboned slippers with a new chalkboard behind her—would be in color. Jessie, a different person at the end of the holiday, would place that photo in the family album and label it "Christmas 1961, Meadow Drive. Charles 9, Charlotte 7."

On New Year's Eve, the three Conrads spent the afternoon and evening at Aunt Ethel's house, where a rich smell of something like molasses and coffee, mixed with dog hair and cigarette smoke, laced each room. The family loved it there, with Ethel's tree full of handmade ornaments of bright yarn; and there was a toy box in the basement with a fire truck that had a ladder that actually raised upward with a toy fireman robot. During each visit they wound the plastic fireman with a key, and he whirred, jerked, and loudly scaled the steps to the top of the ladder. Upstairs Uncle Jacob showed Charles his new fishing rod and tackle. Two presents were under the tree for the children. Ethel gave Jessie a new wall calendar. "I suppose Daddy is holding his New Year's Eve meeting," she said.

Indeed, across the map at his home, Henry was hosting his annual gathering of minds. This, to Henry Hall, was as important as his papers and collections in considering the meaning of life. His longtime friend Navy Halloren and the mayor, Cecil, arrived at seven thirty for their casual debate. They removed their coats and moved with Henry to the parlor on Main Street. Each man lit his pipe, marking the beginning of their shared New Year's Eve ritual.

"Okay, gentlemen." Henry set his hand down on the oak table he had positioned in the center of the room with three chairs.

"Let's put it on the table. This year's topic is Time," he said in serious challenge.

The men sat down on Henry's wingback chairs and grasped their pipes, sending dancing patterns of tobacco smoke into the stratosphere of the room in front of more clocks and guns, giving shape to their thoughts. The men settled into their friendship and the last night of the year.

"I'll begin," Henry said. "I received a letter from Eli Miller, telling me he saw me standing in his room in the middle of the night one night last month, when of course I wasn't ... But it happened to be a night, I recalled, that when I awoke the next morning, I made a note that I felt I had had no sleep at all, as though I had traveled somewhere."

Navy and Cecil raised their eyebrows in great interest and nodded in thoughtful study.

"That is what I wish to discuss regarding Time tonight," Henry said, as though he had laid the first card. "What do you have, Mayor?"

Sweet-smelling smoke continued to rise as the men pulled at the lips of their pipes and exhaled. "About in the summertime," the mayor began, holding his pipe outward, "I had a dream. Well, at the end of the dream, a prominent figure stood facing me in an odd pose, like a military posture, only the man was in civilian clothes. But it was his face that stared forward from that pose, with both hands on his hips. The face with no expression stared straight into my eyes. Then I woke up."

"So?" said Navy.

"Well," Cecil continued, "that day in the mail my issue of *National Geographic* arrived, and on the magazine cover was a man with that face and odd posture. Exactly. I had never seen him before." The mayor took in a slow draw of tobacco. "It should have been the other way around." He squinted. "I should have had the dream *after* seeing the magazine cover." The other men nodded deliberately in agreement.

Navy Halloren knew it was his turn, and after a minute of appreciation, he began slowly. "You both know that my brother passed away in January. End of January. Hmm," he said, looking at them, "almost a year." He cast a quick glance at the clocks on the wall. "Well, you know I cared for him in our house toward the end." He moved in his chair, shifting his weight. "I haven't told anyone this ... but, well, before he died, just before he died, he saw ... people in the room, I guess."

Henry could see that his friend was uncomfortable. "How interesting," he encouraged. "Tell us more."

Navy looked at his good friend in uneasiness. "He ... my brother ... pushed me aside that night, his last night, as I was sitting at his bedside, and he told me to move so he could see her."

"Who?" the two friends asked.

Navy looked down and pushed against his weight in the chair, pausing. "I don't know," he said. "No one else was in the room. I looked to where Richard, my brother, was gazing so steady, but there was nothing there."

"What did you do?"

"I moved. I moved to a chair nearby. Richard continued to gaze—at the air. I asked him what he was looking at. He said, 'Her.' I asked him what she was wearing, and he said, 'A beautiful white gown.'"

Now all three friends, in puzzlement, were uneasy.

Navy looked at them in agreement. "I know. I didn't know what to make of it." He paused, smoking. "There's more. The day before, my brother said there was a group of people in the room. And then ... a dog."

"A dog?" the mayor asked.

"Yeah. Well, this is what is kinda strange. He said the dog was lying next to him. I asked him to describe the dog to me—to just talk with him, you know. This was all new ... and he described the dog."

"And?" Henry said.

"He described his hunting buddy's dog exactly, who had just died the week before."

All of the clocks in the smoky room chimed the hour of eight, each gong winding around and through the men's poised chairs and stilled shoes. "We have much to discuss tonight, gentlemen," Henry said earnestly, purposefully.

CHAPTER 9

arefoot. Much was done barefoot at 147—by Charlotte anyway, even in January. The first Saturday of 1962 arrived with four more inches of snowfall. While Charlotte was waiting for Mrs. Bauer to arrive for her piano lesson, Jessie told Charlotte to get her shoes and go to the piano to get ready. "Until she comes," she said, "why don't you play a hymn from the Christmas book Mrs. Bauer gave to you? Hymns are perfect practice for counting."

Jessie was making beds and now in Charles's room, pulling the bedspread up over his pillow. In the final step, as she pushed the brown and yellow spread under the pillow front and ran the back of her hand down along its crease, while smoothing out the last wrinkle of the woven design of cowboys on horseback and lassos in the air, she thought of Walter, for he had the same bedspread.

Charlotte skipped to the piano and turned to the simple two-hand arrangement of the Dutch hymn "We Gather Together."

She sat at the piano and played it through quite well. Charles was beginning to give up on the piano, but Charlotte could feel its attraction.

When Mary came to the door, snow was still falling on the sturdy rooftops of West Emmette, capping the houses in white hats; the temperature had dropped to 22 degrees. Charlotte, her hair full of static, opened the front door as her mother had instructed.

Mary greeted Charlotte with a happy, loud "Hello!" brightened by the cold air and white background behind her. She had a blue music book in her coat arm and two magazines. She stepped inside enough to close the door behind her, then stepped back onto the cotton rag rug to stomp her boots of snow. "Wooo!" she called out. "Here it comes!"

Mary asked Charlotte to hold her bundle of booklets while she removed her coat and the black rubber boots from over her shoes. She set down her purse, to which the kitten ran up, and Mary said, "Hello, Lucy! It's only me, happy me!" Mary then placed her coat across the old, brown leather chair to her right and took back in hand the new, blue piano book, setting the two used magazines on the table by the chair for Jessie.

"This one is for you!" she said excitedly, walking with Charlotte over to the spinet, just a few steps into the room along the wall. On the plaster wall above the piano hung a piece of artwork Charlotte had made for her mother for Christmas.

Charlotte gazed at the new booklet Mrs. Bauer placed on the piano stand; Mary moved the children's Christmas hymnbook gently aside. The teacher and the girl sat down on the bench beside each other.

"You have progressed to Book B already, Charlotte!" Mary said. "I'm confident you will be able to learn these." Mary turned to the beginning pages. "You see, the songs begin simple enough. In fact, you can probably sight-read through the first song, but we will take our time. Then," she said as she turned the pages forward, "the pieces get a little more challenging."

Charlotte's eyes took in the sight of the pages, which were full of many more notes than she had seen before. The staffs were crammed together with what looked like a threatening shout of tiny black notes joined together with double bars running up and down like birds in flight.

Mary Bauer taught piano the way the John W. Schaum course objectives were listed like laws by number on the book's first page:

1. To teach piano in the most natural and happiest way.
2. To present technical information accurately and progressively.
3. Not to define the scope of Grade I or Grade II or any other grades.
4. Not to confine the intellectual range of the pupil within the 1st year or any other period of time.

Mary said to Charlotte, "We will continue in your scale and theory papers too, Charlotte." She turned to the first song. "In this book, a few songs later, we will learn about chord inversions and how to use the damper pedal. I know it's hard for you to reach the pedals yet, but we'll make it work. Now see if you can sight-read this first song. Take the right hand alone first."

In the kitchen, Jessie listened while packing up the remaining Christmas decorations, giving the three stockings a final hug, and setting them across the filled box of ornaments. After a half hour, as the lesson ended and Charlotte stood, Mary called Jessie to the living room, taking over the piano bench to play a song for the three of them. Mary swung into the keys with speed, bursting forth with the lively notes of "There Is a Tavern in the Town." Jessie, standing behind the bench with Charlotte, joined Mary in singing,

And drinks his wine 'mid laughter free,
And never, never thinks of me!

Charlotte looked up at her mom as they moved into the chorus and tried to sing along.

Fare thee well, for I must leave thee,
Do not let the parting grieve thee.

Mary played the jolly notes by ear, singing loudly, and with the "adieus," she looked back at Charlotte with a nod and great smile, to repeat after her, "Adieu, adieu, kind friends adieu, adieu, adieu!'" And on she played, "And may the world go well with thee," her left hand jumping down the octaves with a C-major broken chord and her right hand signing off with a high and mighty trill. The three girls clapped and laughed as Mary finished.

Putting on her coat, Mary asked Jessie whether she had given thought to the metronome. "It might be helpful, Jessie. Charlotte is doing very well, but a metronome helps a child keep a more correct pace and tempo."

"I'm looking into it," Jessie replied. She was torn by her father's opinion on the subject, and the cost was a factor. "Daddy doesn't have one … and he sort of said he wasn't sure that it was for everyone."

Mary chuckled. "Playing the sax and jazz is very different from classical piano, Jessie. Jazzmen improvise a lot. Classical music is by the book." She paused and added with a touch to Jessie's wrist, "Charlotte tends to rush most songs too."

"Yes, I see. Well, I'm working on it." Jessie said. "What is the cost of the new book?"

"One dollar, Jessie. By the way, Schaum offers a book of ballet music. Maybe one day this year we can look at that too. I brought you a couple of magazines," Mary added, nodding to the table.

Jessie gave her the dollar for the book and one for the lesson, then hugged her friend goodbye.

The lesson list left for the week of practice ahead was, first, a new theory page, then song two in the new blue book, called "Music Box," and also a review of song one. Directions were written in the lesson book below the new reward sticker, that of a cardinal. Mary had also told Charlotte she could make up a song—"sound out a melody"—if she wanted to and also color the drawings above the two lesson songs in the new book.

By Monday West Emmette was blanketed in another fresh three inches of snow on top of its December base. Charlotte, Charles, and the children of the village and township were back in their classrooms below the chimneys and rising columns of steady coal and boiler steam. Math lessons marched on, and spelling tests stacked up until finally Friday was here. The bell rang in Charlotte's room after lunch, when Mrs. Shore said it was time once again for square dancing. Charlotte was now squarely in love with Stevie, who had sent her a real Christmas card in the mail during vacation. Today they were to review the steps of the square dance and practice for the village barn dance, held every May near the end of the school year in farmer Owens's barn.

Square-dance class took place in the long cafeteria room, where at its back wall a stage had been built after the war. Charlotte loved lining up in her classroom and filing to the stage for the dance hour. She still loved to dance. Loved it. She missed the ballet exercises she had been introduced to during the two years before her dad's accident. Now this was fun too. Mrs. Shore was reviewing the steps for the children after turning on the record player in the corner. Mrs. Shore did not look like a dancer. She looked more like a baker. But she leaned into her duty with her block black shoes and pudgy legs, looking through her thick black glasses set on a lemon-drop nose, and called out the order of steps.

"Remember, first we bow to our partner, then bow to our corner, go forward and back, circle left, promenade, swing our partner, allemande left, then promenade again," she said, moving singly and swiftly about the floor to the pointed-out "square," smiling in the hour as though she were dancing with God.

The children awaited their turns in wooden chairs lined up at the back of the stage floor. "Okay! Let's pair up!" Mrs. Shore called out with a clap.

Here it was. Fate in full force. Mrs. Shore paired her children alphabetically, taking the "A" girl with the "Z" boy, the "B" girl with the "V" or "W" boy. Charlotte Conrad was often paired with Stevie Thomas, and, joining hands again, they stepped forward into their place in the square. And the *clap, clap, stomp, stomp* flight of square dancing swung into a wonderful flurry of loops and circles below clasps of hands and giggles all around the stage.

Meanwhile, toward the center of the school building, Charles was taking his turn in the grade school bookstore, working the noon-to-one-o'clock shift at the thick, richly grained oak sales window in a dim corner somewhere in a hall that seemed mysteriously removed from authority and lessons. While waiting for any fellow student customers, Charles wasn't one to stack the pink erasers and yellow tablets or even appreciate the wondrous smell of pencil lead and lined paper and imagination. Instead, he leaned into the open oak window frame, which by this decade was deeply smoothed into a dark, black-brown color by time and years of skin oil, examining its hinge and latch. A bracket was loose, so when Mr. Shipp, the custodian, walked by, Charles asked him about it. "Do you have a screwdriver handy?" Charles said.

Maxwell Shipp stopped in his track, his tools still moving forward but then swinging back to an obedient pause above the master's boots. "How do you do? I'm Mr. Shipp." He shook

Charles's hand. "Mr. Powell and I are on our way down to the basement to look for an extra desk and chair. Want to come along? We'll get the right screwdriver."

Charles happily closed and locked the store window and exited the side of the aromatic supply closet. "Sure!" he said and followed Mr. Shipp to the office door, where they picked up Mr. Powell and walked to the stairwell opposite the cafeteria.

Mr. Shipp led the way down the great gray steps. Charles followed, with Mr. Powell behind him. At the base of the stairwell, to the left of the small concrete landing, was a metal, green-painted door with a large silver-ball knob. As Mr. Shipp pulled open the heavy door, it creaked in its metal hinge, and he held it open for the two visiting men. "I need to oil that today," he said to Mr. Powell.

The great old furnace, the same one that had heated the building when Charles's dad was a student there, rumbled loudly on this cold winter day and dutifully poured hot air through the channels of air ducts above, sending heat up to the classrooms, cafeteria, hallways, and great slate chalkboards. Charles could hear water running softly to the boiler in the copper lines along the sides of the ceiling above their heads.

Max Shipp led Charles over to his toolbox and explained that he was building a new workbench.

Mr. Powell saw the glow in Charles's expression. "Mr. Shipp is a fine craftsman and handyman, Charles. Any time you have a question, just ask him." The men nodded to each other, both looking to help the young lad without a father.

Meanwhile, over the school's flat roof, over the elementary classrooms, where chalk skated methodically across blackboards with the week's closing lessons, more new snow continued to fall straight down in a rush, adding two more inches of white surface to the January terrain. At the township's high school, two miles down the road, teacher Warren Buckley, at the end of his algebra class, stepped out of his classroom door onto an attached porch exit and looked down at his shoes. He went to the school office to use the phone.

"Scott? This is Warren. What do you say we barricade Meadow Drive for sledding tonight?" he said into the phone to Chief Briicker. "Snow's perfect."

"What?"

"Over in Paxton we used to close Maple Street for the kids. It was great. Meadow would be perfect, you know."

"Well ... let me talk to the mayor. I guess we could put a barricade at the top. I could park the squad car up there. There's not much traffic after six anyway." He pondered. "We'll need someone at the bottom."

"Carver has a construction horse. I've already talked to Bowler. And Paul will be home. That's the majority of the council. We'll all be there. Paul can watch the bottom."

Warren drove to his home on Meadow Drive after school and walked over to Braunhall's house. Braunhall was shoveling his driveway. "We might close Meadow tonight for sledding," he told his neighbor. "Scott is checking with the mayor."

Carver Braunhall immediately went into the garage, pulled out two sawhorses, and lifted down a sled from a peg on the wall. "Tommy! Get out here!" he called. His son emerged from the kitchen door. "Get your brother. We need to wax these runners. Get some wax paper."

Tommy looked up at Warren. "Hi, Mr. Buckley."

"Hi, Tommy." He looked at the son of the drinking man.

"Where are we going?" Tommy asked his father.

"Sledding! Right here!"

Warren Buckley went to the Simmons' and Bowlers' houses, then went home, checked with Scott, who said Cecil agreed; then he called the pharmacist. "Coyne, what time will you be home?"

"Six," Paul answered.

"Good." Warren told his friend that the road closing was confirmed. "We'll see you and Junior. We're thinking seven o'clock. Bring home a few bandages, maybe, and some … I don't know. Iodine. Whatever."

"Good idea. I will," his friend replied.

At seven o'clock a light snow was still falling on the village. The several weeks of steady cold and snow had settled into a solid base on the street, which was never salted and only plowed. That day's car tires had packed the new snow surface down to a two-inch-dense snowpack, grayed over the weeks by time and travel. Chief Briicker halted plowing after Warren called and then made several drives down the street himself at 6:45 to further pack down the snow base before parking his patrol car at the top of the street, where Meadow ended at Midville. He parked his blue and white car facing the street downward, letting his headlights light up the top of the hill. Carver placed his two sawhorses across the street at the lower bend, and he and Raymond Jones joined the group.

Voices and laughter started to rise in a muffle in the dark, snow-filled air at the top of Meadow Drive with the arrival of sleds—pulled and carried to the top of the street, which was right in front of Charles and Charlotte's driveway.

There was, of course, a knock on the Conrad door. It was Jackie. "C'mon! C'mon!" he yelled at them. "Everybody's sledding down Meadow!" And off he flew to join the neighbors at the street top.

Charles needed only to turn around. Jessie had already grabbed his coat, hat, and gloves. Charlotte began to run about the house, looking for hers. "She's not coming!" Charles yelled.

"Oh, yes, she is," Jessie said calmly. "You look after her, Charles."

Charlotte plunked down on the kitchen floor with her thick socks and boots, and grabbed her snow hat and coat from the rack at the back door. Their sleds were in the garage. No time to wax the runners first.

Out the two went into the snowy night. Jessie turned on her single-bulb front porch lamp to add a little more light to the wintry Friday night. She opened the front interior door to peer outside through the cold storm door glass, which steamed quickly from the burst of breath and contrasting warm air that hit it. She rubbed a patch clear on the glass with her hand to see that all the other porch lights were on, and the street was filled with small, puffy coats and some other large, thick coats. Warren Buckley was directing the sledding push offs at the top of the street, letting only one or two children go down at a time, one after another.

When Charles and Charlotte reached the end of their driveway and approached the group, they saw Jackie and Bobby who, like soldiers armed for battle, were running with their sleds held like shields before them, and in their turn they slapped the sleds down in a hurried clap and in the same breath threw their coat buttons down onto the length of those wooden sled boards. Down the street they flew, the sleds' metal runners cutting quick down the hill into the dark below.

Charles and Charlotte's sleds were their parents' childhood sleds. Charles had his dad's Fire Fly sled, a slightly longer version than Charlotte's. The wood was a bit dry and the name worn, but the steering column was just fine. Real fine, in fact. His dad's name was even carved into the bottom board underneath. Charlotte had never gone down a hill by herself. Her dad had only pulled her on this sled in their yard or on their flat sidewalk. She wasn't sure what to do with it.

Charles helped Charlotte put her sled down on the transformed road and told her quickly what to do. Charlotte's heart pounded, but she tried to appear unafraid. Charles was at her side, and what he said, she did.

"Now look, Charlotte," her brother said. "Keep your hands on this top bar here and keep the rope up, and when you run, you jump on. Okay?"

Suddenly, Charlotte started to cry. She glanced at the other sleds flying down the street to a dark distance. Charles looked up at Mr. Buckley and looked back down at his sister. "All right," Charles said. "Here," he told Charlotte. "You get on my back, okay? I'll show you how." He started to position his sled on the slippery surface, holding it in place. "Sir," he asked, "would you help Charlotte get on my back and give us a push?"

Charlotte quickly set her sled over off the road in their driveway and climbed onto her brother's back. She hooked her booted feet around his legs and grabbed his puffed arms with her mittens. Mr. Buckley helped her.

"Hold on to my coat real tight," Charles shouted back. "Ready? Okay!" He gripped the crossbar, and Mr. Buckley reached down and gave the pair a careful, solid push forward.

The sled slid its weight forward down the street, its steel runners gliding nicely over the padded white surface. The few sleds before them had begun to form a slick, carved path, and Charles's sled stayed in those tracks. Charles gazed forward with squinted eyes into the rushing snowflakes, his face just over the snow-packed road as they picked up speed. Charlotte was still on his back, grasping his sleeves in the tightest grip. Charles held his buckled boots up off the road behind them, his toes bumping down now and then to the path. He'd need to work on that, he thought.

On they rode, past the Leskoviches', Joneses', and Braunhalls' houses; and Charles heard Charlotte giggling with excitement over his hat. Another house, two, three; then they were approaching the bend. Charles saw Mr. Coyne and the few other kids at the bend and began to drag his boot toes down hard in the street to slow the sled down, just as he had read to do in the *Boys' Life* magazine article last December. They passed Jackie and Mitch and two other boys at the end of the run, who all shouted "Ho!" at them and ran to meet them as their sled came to a stop. "Hurry! Clear the road! Here comes Rooster!"

Charlotte rolled off Charles's coat and slid down onto the snow, where Mr. Coyne helped her up.

"Good job, Charlotte!" Mr. Coyne said joyfully, lifting the yarn-hatted girl upright to her feet. "Good job too, Charles! You two came down fast!"

Charlotte, a little dazed, smiled up through the snowflakes at him and said, "Thank you." She looked at her brother, and the word "Again?" wasn't even asked. They each grabbed a side of the old rope loop on the sled and started to trek back up the hill, walking on the left-side lawns, where the other sleds had created a return path. Mrs. Leskovich also was watching from her front window at the trudges through her front yard.

When the other children saw how fast Charles and Charlotte went down together with the double weight, they formed pairs too and rode piggyback down the hill. Others sat up on their sleds, steering with their feet; and on their fifth run, Charles tried that method with Charlotte sitting behind him.

Sleds were piling up at the Conrad driveway post lamp, and Jessie watched the action from her bedroom window, which offered the best view of the street. She sat down at her desk there, below the double-hung window, and opened a drawer to take out her box of new greeting cards. She needed to address two birthday cards for Monday's mail. She lifted through the various greetings, all lovely in their illustrations, with pastel colors and scrolled lettering. She turned up two get-well cards, a sympathy card, and an anniversary card before coming to the birthday cards, each of them three inches by six. She chose two with thoughtful prose, then addressed and signed them with love in her petite, well-schooled script. All Jessie's friends admired her pleasant, dainty penmanship.

At eight thirty Jessie went to the front door in the living room and flipped the porch switch on and off a few times to tell her two children it was time to come in. Soon she heard the side garage door bang open and the sleds bump their way to the side wall; then boots stomped across the garage and up the steps into the kitchen landing. The brother and sister were crowned in white snow and frost, their jackets and pants packed with snow cover. They stopped on the rug inside the door to pull off their boots, barely able to bend down or move. Jessie helped Charlotte pull off her black boots—formerly her brothers'.

"Where should we go?" Charles asking, dripping ice. His face was red with cold, and his socks were wet and toes numb. But he was full of joy and satisfaction.

"My toes hurt," Charlotte said to her mother in amazement. Her feet felt disconnected from her body as she looked down at her red toes.

"Downstairs," Jessie said to Charles, smiling. "Why don't we go downstairs."

The three stepped over the four dropped boots and slowly marched, with ice dripping down the basement stairs, to the gray stationary tub and clothesline beside the washing machine. There they unzipped and dropped their jackets and snow pants, snow falling in blotches to the old rug there. A floor drain was three feet away and under the tub to catch the melt.

Jessie draped the snow pants and jackets over the washtub and on the clothesline tied over it; she placed their gloves across the tub divide, then hung their hats and scarves on the other clothesline behind them.

Charlotte's small feet and toes were turning white when she and her brother marched back upstairs in their underwear; her feet would remain freshly stiff with cold for another half hour, even while they sipped hot chocolate and watched some of the *Bell Telephone Hour* show on TV in her bathrobe before crawling under the electric blankets Aunt Ethel had given to all three for Christmas.

That winter night in the center of town, Henry Marshall Hall was repairing a French mantel clock. He removed three pins and a screw from the back plate, then let the striking and timing springs down. With long, special tweezers, he knowingly removed the wheels, the striking train, and the two barrels, then noticed a bad pivot on one wheel. He would repair that tomorrow. He glanced at the bowl of spare clock keys to his side, turned his stool away from the parts set in careful sequence on his desktop, and opened a drawer, taking out a notebook.

With a pen he noted in his log that the black walnut, weight-driven 1875 Regulator No. 6 Seth Thomas clock and the Gustav Becker clock would be given to Ethel and Jessie upon his death. Due to events and obligations over the years, he found himself always planning ahead. He flipped a few pages back in the journal to where he had begun making notes for his obituary and where he had listed the songs to be played at his funeral. "Old Kentucky Home" was one. He leaned back and reflected aloud. "I am a lucky man," he said to himself as a warm tingle rose to his thin chest.

His eyes were drawn to his wife's face in her portrait on the wall to his side. She was so beautiful, he thought. He looked more deeply into the shadowed image, at Elizabeth's succumbing profile, looking out the window toward her fate. Her sad but accepting eyes, her lovely chin, her caring hand holding the heavy curtain to a part, as the photographer had suggested, letting the window light illuminate only her face, her strong nose, her white lace collar, the front of her dark-brown hair, pulled back into a heavy coil of braid, which disappeared into the darkness of the shadowed curtain and room behind her. He thought of the clipping of her hair, which he kept in the emptied Jack Straws box.

And there in the frame next to Elizabeth's was the portrait of his mother, the most beautiful woman he had ever known. Soft spoken, wise. There was great wisdom in her face. Plain hair parted down the middle, her head turned to the future. There was a little bit of Indian in the shape of her mouth. Her eyes, brows, and face were healthy, strongly proportioned. He leaned closer, seeing a small resemblance in Charlotte. His mother was wearing a high-buttoned, dark dress, her hands crossed on her lap, and she held a lovely, large handkerchief with the tip of her right fingers, her left hand showing fingernails worn short from work. What was that around her neck—a long ornate band, holding a ... whistle? *Whatever happened to that necklace?* he wondered.

He looked around the room for a better place to file his papers. On his desk he shuffled the book manuscript, his upcoming speech for the St. David's Society, the photo from Harvey Field, the clipping about the 1960 Pirates game ... and his letter to his daughters.

CHAPTER 10

S pring approached in April, and Charlotte was counting down the days until her eighth birthday. The mayor was attending the ornithology convention in Pittsburgh, and Bill and Simon were preparing to dig and mold more soil at their newly named Simon's Grove Swim Park.

Moons rose and set toward the month of May, and Henry stood with Mayor Grisby one morning at the lake site, arms crossed, watching Bill and Simon resume work on the property.

"Do you think this is a good idea?" Cecil asked Henry.

"I sure do," Henry answered. "The kids need a safe place to swim." The two watched the men clear a few more trees on the north end of the property. "Did you hear that the Catholic church is planning to build a parsonage now?"

"I heard," Cecil said. The Reverend Father Parker had been renting a house on Main Street five doors down from the post office. "They've held picnics and dances and fish fries, spaghetti dinners, raffles and now bingo even. Everything they can possibly do to raise money to pay for that church."

"Interesting. They sure have moved in. Two hundred fifty members now, I think," Henry said.

"Well, the members of the church built a fine structure. I guess the Zimmers will build the parsonage. It's going to be behind the little pond to the side of the church, on the Arbor Road side."

"How was the meeting in Pittsburgh?" Henry asked.

"Great. We're going to start a bird count. Log the number of bluebirds and cardinals we see the rest of this month for the next meeting," Cecil answered. "I saw a cedar waxwing this morning."

"Don't know I've ever seen one," Henry commented.

"I wonder what kind of season the Pirates will have this year," Cecil began, then he changed the subject. "I was in the audience the other night," he said.

"At the Ohio gun collectors' conference?" Henry asked.

"Yeah. Very interesting. You made good points about the identification of John Shell rifles."

"Do you have one?"

"No, but a friend does, and he's always referred to it as being a Kentucky John Shell." Cecil paused. "Listen, Double H, there was a guy there. This man—he seemed out of place. Seemed sort of nervous. He seemed a little put out or something. You see anyone like that?"

Henry knew the man his friend was speaking of. Again, it was Jace. "Yes, I've seen him before, Cecil. He's got a bug in his mind. He doesn't like it that I have the Rupp rifle. He's Harvey Field's son. He thinks his daddy should have given the gun to him, not to me. His dad was one of my best friends at the ordnance. And before. Son has a problem. Anyway, Harvey didn't think Jace could keep a gun."

"He bother you?"

"Nah. He just shows up at talks sometimes. Lives out on County Line Road now, on his mother's property. Feel kind of sorry for him."

"Where's his dad now—your friend?"

"He passed away four … maybe four or five years ago in Virginia. He helped me with my rifle history book, you know. He had a collection too. A pretty big collection. Gave me the Rupp rifle after the war."

Bill and Simon's tractor and bulldozer moved into higher gear, happily crisscrossing the land with more smoke.

"I hear you're going to speak to the school kids next week," Cecil said.

"Yeah, about camping, wildlife conservation, scouting … and again about the role of the rifle in pioneer days. Also, from the book, that the Kentucky rifle was really made in Lancaster County, Pennsylvania. Probably some of their families came from there."

"Yep," Cecil said, well familiar with the book. "So listen, we're moving forward with the Lions Club. It's part of our township duty, you know. Want to head it up?"

"Nah. Let one of the younger guys do it."

"How about Luther?"

"Too busy."

"Kenny?"

"Maybe. Hope he's interested."

"I'll approach him. There'll be time to put some men together over the summer for a Thanksgiving drive. The charter says a good way to start the club is meals for the needy."

"No one around here will accept a meal, Mayor."

"I know. But we'll find some families. They're out there."

"Shaw family."

"Clothes too maybe, for them."

Henry and Cecil watched Bill hop off of his tractor to move a turtle, waved a goodbye to him, and got back in their cars. Henry thought about the Field son, Jace, wondering whether he might need some meals.

He drove down Main Street, where the elm trees were in full bloom and providing their beautiful shade and canopy over the street he loved, thinking of the brick below this generation's pavement and the day he and his bride had moved there. He pulled into his gravel driveway across from the school. It was close to 2:45, and Jessie sat in her Corvair in the extended lot, ready for school dismissal and crossing duty. They waved at each other. Henry kissed his hand and touched it in the air to her.

Henry entered his back door and could smell a pot of cooked rhubarb cooling on the stovetop. Ada wasn't there now, however. He took some chamomile tea from the refrigerator and walked toward the parlor. Bird was lying on his backboard, an oak plank sloped slightly head down on the floor, stretching his long back for relief. The men nodded to each other, and Henry continued on to his study across from the living room, where his clocks were ticking softly together in nap. He would wake them momentarily to wind a few. Breathing in and out, in and out, Henry gauged himself steadily as he wound each clock, being careful to not hold his breath, which he sometimes found himself doing in concentration.

Finishing, he took an arrowhead in his hand in his pocket, feeling its smooth history in his roughened but well-groomed fingertips as he paused in peace at the last clock face. He glanced over at his slender rifles, thinking of the day at the feed mill when Gallagher had first come to his desk and asked him to go to Cleveland to serve in the arms division as chief inspector. It had been 1942, and the United States was moving into war. Jessie and Matthew were engaged.

Tick, tick.

The Allan Fowlds clock chimed three in E major.

During the war, Jessie married Matthew after he had been discharged from the army for a heart murmur, and after the war they moved to Columbus. Ethel had married Jacob Cohler, and they still lived one town over. Even though the two sisters grew up without a mother, both girls somehow learned to keep tidy, if not simple, homes.

Tick, tick.

Henry listened to the multi-level measure of time in his room. The Barnes Bartholomew clock lay open on his desktop. He needed one part from Cleveland before re-assembling it for Vince next door. What was that Vince had said during their last chat, as they talked over the dog resting at their feet? That's right. He mentioned Jace too. Said Jace had asked Vince a question about him.

Vince and Ada rather shared the vet's dog, Chimney. Chimney was back and forth between their two porches all day long. The dog oddly liked carrots, and Ada had no shortage for him. Chimney was a smart, little dog. Maybe it was time for him to get his own dog again too.

Tick, tick.

Bird appeared in the doorway, paintbrush in hand, and said he was going back over to the job on Lilac. It was nice for Bird to have paint jobs in town now after the many years of his driving to the city.

Later that night a storm moved in with high winds from the west and pounding rain. On Meadow, Charlotte crawled into bed with her mom, and Heidi hid under Charles's bed; and on Main Street, Chimney stayed in with Vince, his master.

When Henry opened his eyes the next morning, his head deep and still in the old down pillow, an assembly of strange words came to him: "The twelve birds were calling together.

'Why are we here?' the captain said." These words played vividly
and instantly across the screen of Henry's mind. He repeated them
once, lying on his pillow, wondering why those words would be
joined together, and he wrote them down on his nightstand pad
when he sat up.

It was Saturday morning. The storm had moved on, and in
town, boots strolled, and truck tires rolled toward the barbershop,
pharmacy, and soda fountain counter. Men in their hunting
khakis and farming jeans talked about the new addition being
planned by the Hartmans. With Paul Coyne's blessing, Violet and
Roy were going to turn the back end of the pharmacy building
into a small restaurant. Bicycles darted out of driveways, crossing
Main Street and Meadow and Thistle; other bikes dropped by the
schoolyard ball field.

Ada called Henry to the kitchen for breakfast. Bird was
already there. Ada placed bowls of hot oatmeal on the small oak
table in the corner. "Smells great," Henry said, moving calmly
to the worn, notched table at the right side of the kitchen room.
Each of the three family members shared a few comments about
the storm; then the three ate quietly from the chipped china
bowls, only their spoons making an occasional light clink. They
were comfortable with each other, settled into a routine of age
and harmony on the quiet, old street.

"Did you stop the Fowlds clock during the night?" Henry
asked his sister. He knew that one clock's deep roaring chime
bothered Ada.

"No. I did not. Why?" she asked.

"Well, the clock stopped."

"Had you just wound it?" she asked. "Too tight maybe? Did
you check the level?" She knew Henry never wound the clocks
too tightly and always checked the levels.

"Yes, I checked the level. It is not off center."

"Oh," Ada said. She thought of the ghost. "What time did it stop at?"

"Five thirty. The clock read five thirty when I came down this morning."

Ada was relieved. Or disappointed maybe. She knew it wouldn't be the ghost, not at five thirty. "Could it be the storm?" she asked.

"No." Henry felt concern but didn't express it to Ada and Bird. Bird said nothing. He tolerated the noise of Henry's clocks but wasn't interested in them.

Henry thought it suspicious that the Fowlds clock should stop. It just never would, and he felt a little sick inside. Before turning in last night, he had walked through his parlor past the well-buffed rifles, past the bookcase and his pipe rack, past each clock—and looked into the face of the Allan Fowlds clock, made in Kilmarnock. He'd taken his handkerchief from his pocket to wipe a spot of dust. The handkerchief had dislodged his pocket watch, which fell down on the gold chain to his pant leg, he recalled. He had grasped the heavy, smooth, gold disc and set it in his palm to look at it. It read ten o'clock. The clock's time matched his watch, correct to the minute. He had wound the watch's top dial to give it another day of running. The Scottish pendulum of the Fowlds clock had swung in perfect rhythm then, its brass weights above midheight. Putting his watch back in his pocket, Henry had walked to the kitchen and back door to make sure Ada had locked it. Chimney wasn't on the porch—he was apparently back over at Vince's, knowing rain was approaching.

That morning at 147, after Charlotte's piano lesson, Jessie gathered her checkbook and Social Security check from her right top desk drawer and took Charles and Charlotte in their Corvair to the Metropolitan Bank in Benton twenty minutes away. This was a big monthly trip. The three Conrads entered the formal, important glass doors of the bank in a new plaza. Charles and Charlotte stood by their mother as she deposited two checks from the school and this month's Social Security check, and she kept sixty dollars in cash.

She then led Charles forward to the teller and told the woman her son would like to open his own savings account. Charles pulled fourteen dollars from his pocket; the money was from birthday gifts and earned from his new newspaper route, passed on to him by Butch.

He placed the cash on the woman's counter. The teller's posture stiffened with earnest pleasure, and she commented on his success; she counted out the money, then gave Charles a little booklet, explaining to him how his deposits would be logged. He would earn 3.75 percent in interest on his savings. With this year's fair and another knickknack in mind, Charlotte was keeping her dimes and nickels in the tin globe bank her father had given her.

Afterward the family stopped at a hardware store next to the bank, then drove over to the new McDonald's fast-food restaurant, where the yellow arches were at the main intersection of Market and Benton Streets, at the top of the busy intersection above the new plaza and theater. Charles and Charlotte loved the sweet, flat hamburgers and crispy french fries, but they had no idea—no idea—how much their mother relished this meal with a chocolate milkshake. If the banking was a frightful worry and always foreboding, this little meal out in their Corvair was a reward. It was great, great fun—a luxury paid for with her school crossing guard money.

Charles saved two fries for Heidi, and when they got home, he called to his dog. Heidi was looking a few pounds overweight, as was Charles. Aunt Ethel noticed this issue and commented on it to her sister that afternoon.

"Jessie, I see that Charles is putting on a few extra pounds for a boy his age," she said.

"I know, Ethel. I don't know how to help it right now. He's so quiet sometimes, you know. He's still adjusting." Jessie paused. "You know, Emma told me that Walter has gained a few pounds too."

"How about Charlotte?" Ethel asked. "She seems happy."

"Yeah, Charlotte has a good, little imagination. She draws a lot. She drew a picture the other day of herself and Walter. I had to ask her who it was." Jessie chuckled. "Dad's coming over for dinner tonight. You and Jacob want to come? We won't eat until six."

"Sure. What can I bring?"

"Oh, I don't know. How about a green bean casserole? I'd better get busy. We went to the bank this morning, and I didn't bake."

"Skip it!" her sister said.

"I guess I'll have to. I'll keep dinner simple," Jessie agreed.

At five o'clock Jessie asked Charlotte to set the table. "Use the china. Be careful, honey. There'll be six of us. Aunt Ada and Uncle Bird aren't coming."

When everyone sat down to dinner that evening, Henry said to Charles, "So tomorrow morning when you're delivering newspapers, Charles, don't throw any in the bushes. And Charlotte, don't clip the cartoons in the rotogravure."

Charles looked surprised. "I won't. But why?" he asked.

"I'm going to be in the paper tomorrow."

"What?" Ethel exclaimed.

"In the rotogravure!" Henry said with more fun. "A reporter came over a few weeks ago and has been working on a feature about my clocks. The paper decided to put it in Sunday's special photo section. I'm anxious to see it."

"Oh my!" Jessie said, wondering why Martin McMillan hadn't mentioned it. They were keeping it a surprise, she guessed, humored. "How exciting!"

"A toast!" Ethel's husband, Jacob, said, raising his glass of water. "A toast to our historian!"

And the six set about enjoying their meat and potatoes dinner together. Jessie had made Aunt Mae's baked dinner casserole, a recipe from the woman who had cared for her and Ethel while growing up. She'd added Ethel's side dish and dinner rolls. Charlotte put a lot of margarine on her roll.

While the sisters cleared the table, Henry asked Charlotte to play a duet on the piano with him. Later, as the women were doing dishes in the kitchen, Henry went to his daughters at the sink and leaned his head between them. He said to Jessie, "It's wonderful you got the piano for the kids."

"Thanks, Dad," Jessie said, reaching to tap his hand on her shoulder.

"A piano gives an even voice to everyone," he continued. "No accent. No opinion. Just a … song."

Henry returned to the living room, where Jacob was reading the newspaper sports section. Henry knew Charles had a show-and-tell day coming up for the end of the school year, and he approached Charles, who was playing marbles with Charlotte. Henry reached into his pocket for his watch.

"Here," he said, handing it to Charles. "You can take this to show-and-tell at school. Just take good care of it. I know you will." He looked at the watch fondly. "Remember what I told you about it."

"Yessir," Charles said cautiously. "Gee, Grandpa, thank you." Surprised, Charles held the beautiful gold watch and chain in his growing hands, staring at it and feeling its weight.

"I wouldn't show the engraving in class," Henry said. "But you can tell them it is a gold Elgin. What I told you before."

On Sunday morning the farmers' plows were parked and silent. The Bauers' strawberry plants, already six inches tall, would enjoy a quiet day of growth under their straw and a warming, spring sun. Bill's bulldozer sat still along the pit, which was filling a little with natural water and appearing like a budding lake. The men would now work on creating a sloping beach area. Turtles stepped into the edge of pooled water and disappeared below the calm surface, while the rising sun slowly crawled onto the clocks on Henry's parlor wall. It was six thirty.

Charles and his mom drove through town to the five streets of Charles's new newspaper route; Charles jumped out every few houses with each subscriber's paper, dashing to the doors of his customers. The morning was cool. On their way home, they stopped at the grocery store, newly open on Sundays until one o'clock, to get more dinner rolls. They saw Martin, the door boy, who was whistling in his work of opening up the store.

Once home, they eagerly opened their own newspaper to the rotogravure. Inside the oversized, brown-hued special section, four pages long, in the center fold was a large photo of Henry, their dad and grandfather, in a beautiful portrait with his clocks. There were four photos and captions in all, telling of his collection. In the main photo, over his shoulder, was the Rupp rifle beside the Metzger rifle, leaning against his cherrywood bookcase. Charlotte, Charles and Jessie were filled with pride. The phone rang. It was Ethel.

"Yes, we see it. Isn't it grand?" Jessie answered into the receiver. "Yes, we'll see you in church."

Handshaking was excited and vivid among the friends at church. Members anxiously and happily gathered around Jessie, Ethel, Charles, and Charlotte as they approached the entrance, walking around them toward the door and commenting on their father's feature in the rotogravure. But when the noisy, spirited group reached the church stoop in the fresh spring morning, as birds chirped in the alcove above and perched on the rooftop, everyone spotted Chief Briicker arrive in his patrol car, parking oddly close to the church doorway at the top of the lot.

When he stepped from his car, he looked at Jessie and Ethel. The church members who were in the parking lot lingered nervously nearby to see why Scott was there and what the news was. Mr. Witner, a deacon of the church council, stepped past Scott and the sisters at the doorway, and quickly went into the church to pull the minister outside, to be available. Everything— the moment, the hour—went into black and white again for Jessie.

"Jessie," Scott said. "Ethel. Can I talk to you?" He removed his heavy-rimmed hat with its federal star badge and offered a gentle smile. Patrolman Raymond Jones slowly pulled into the church driveway too.

The sisters stepped down together for another page of their story. They held hands, just as they had when approaching uncertainty throughout their school years. Jessie had motioned for Charles and Charlotte to stay back on the porch with Mrs. Leonard and the minister, recognizing the scene to be serious.

"Jessie, Ethel," Scott began as he took their shoulders after they walked bravely to him from the church steps. His height gave his arms the reach of a cross. "Your daddy had a heart attack, or a stroke. Ada is with him. He's resting at home. He doesn't want to go to the hospital," he said as quietly as possible, though somehow his words reached everyone's ears across the church parcel.

Jessie looked steadily into Scott's eyes in appreciation, though she wondered why it was Scott who had come to tell them. The two sisters returned briefly to Charles and Charlotte, asked them to stay with the minister and his wife, gave them each a kiss on the forehead, and got into Ethel's car to drive to Main Street.

"Wait," the police chief called out. Jessie and Ethel paused, turning back to their classmate. "There's more," he said as he stepped to their car window. "Someone broke into your dad's house last night. About five thirty. Ada said they heard the noise, and your dad started down the stairs to check the house, and he had the attack and collapsed there. On the stairs."

Out on County Line Road, down an overgrown and abandoned orchard lane, near the border of section thirty-five, far outside the village and close to the state line, on the Field farm about four miles from the church door, Jace Field sat behind his grandfather's leaning shed on a weathered bench, clutching the Rupp rifle tightly in his right arm. He was rocking slowly forward and back, forward and back—opposite the swing of a pendulum—eyes clamped shut in the risen morning haze, seeing the scene over and over.

He hadn't meant for Henry to die. Over and over, he saw Henry slump on the stairs, yelling out at him. "Henry saw me," Jace said to himself, sitting in sweat. "Henry saw it was me." He heard Henry's scream in his mind again. Then he heard the thud and the roll down the stairs. He heard himself run back out of the house through the kitchen. He heard the kitchen door slam.

So did Ada. She had heard the door and rushed to the top of the stairs in her nightgown. "Henry!" Jace heard her cry out.

Ada had dashed down the steps to her brother, grabbing his nightshirt, turning him to face upward in the dim light of the hallway. Henry could see his study door from the floor where he had landed and reached toward it. He could speak, but he didn't tell Ada whom he had seen.

"Get me in there," he had said to her in a hushed voice. Bird was then by Ada's side, and the two of them lifted Henry to the small settee on the far wall of the warm room, the reading bench below the oak-framed high, horizontal window, where an owl sat quietly in the oak tree just beyond.

"I'll go get Vince," Bird said, running out the door for their neighbor.

"Let me call the hospital," Ada pleaded to Henry. "Bird can drive you to the hospital." She knew the words she spoke would not be heeded.

Henry shook his head. "No. Just let me rest here."

Soon the door slammed again, and the vet was beside his friend. "What did you do now?" he said gently in the early morning in a hushed, deep voice, opening his bag. He withdrew his stethoscope. Vince could hear a heartbeat that was fainter, even as the clocks around them ticked more loudly. He checked Henry's mouth and gums; the color was pale. He checked the pupils of his eyes. He held Henry's wrist and counted his pulse.

Henry offered a weak smile back, looking at his friend, then closed his eyes in weariness. His body was tired. The pain had been sharp and swift. His arm still felt ... it didn't feel ... he couldn't feel his trigger hand.

Ada said to Vince, "Someone was in the house." She looked at him earnestly. "That's why Henry fell ... had an attack, if he did."

"Yes, I'd guess he had a heart attack, Ada," Vince said. "It could be a stroke." He removed the stethoscope from his neck and set it back in his bag. "I can't tell for sure."

"Someone broke in," Ada said again desperately. "We heard the door."

"Did you see him, Henry?" Vince asked.

Henry's eyes remained closed; he was thinking of Jace, seeing the young man with the rifle in wild grasp, who had turned to look at Henry on the staircase. And in his panic Jace had swung the forty-four-inch rifle barrel into the 1745 Allan Fowlds clock case, smashing the glass. He also had the box.

"No," Henry answered. "No. I saw someone, but I couldn't see who."

"Which gun?" Vince asked.

"You know." Then he drifted into sleep.

Ada gasped. "Is he ... is he breathing?"

"Yes, yes, Ada. He's okay for now," Vince answered. "Just sleeping. Let him sleep. Want him to go to the hospital?"

"He said no."

Vince smiled, knowing that would be the case. "He can rest here. We'll get Dr. Cromwell as soon as I can reach him."

"What should I do for Henry?" Ada asked.

"Let him rest."

❅ ❅ ❅

During the next two weeks, while berry trees blossomed and the elm trees bloomed into their great, green canopy over Main Street, draped by the flights of robins, Jessie and Ethel tended to their dad along with Ada, Bird, Ruby, and Dr. Cromwell, whose office was just four doors away. Henry remained weak, and his spirit seemed to fade. He sat in his study day after day, spending hours slowly logging more and more data, eating less and less. The police chief and Raymond had visited him twice, trying to get more information, determined to recover the gun. By the second visit, Henry seemed resolved. "Never mind, Scott. It's gone. We don't know who came. The rifle is gone. I can live without it."

But could he live without the box of Elizabeth's beautiful hair locks and the broken clock from Kilmarnock? Without the rhythm of that one, singular pendulum, Henry's day lacked order; he felt confused. His own heartbeat was uneven and lost. *Who was right?* he thought over and over. Henry pondered each night, each day. *Who was wrong? It was my gun. I know it,* he thought. *Jace's daddy gave it to me. I have the letter. But I knew Jace wanted it. I couldn't give it up. It meant more to me. But Jace … Jace said he wanted it. But did he have to take the Jack Straws box?*

It was the last week of May. The bees had awakened and were buzzing with new flurry in and out of their great tree knot. The rotogravure page was taped to the wall behind Henry's desk.

There he stood in the photo, in his beloved study, surrounded by his notebooks and his clocks; and in the photo, the gun was still lodged in its rack.

Henry felt tired. Only three o'clock. The house ... Ada was opening her cotton-soaked bag of coffee beans. It smelled good. Henry lay down on the settee, thinking, resting his eyes.

In the kitchen, Ada noticed something. An odd stillness. The clocks were still ticking, keeping their time, but the rooms seemed still. Still and ... heavy. There was a heaviness in the air. Chimney, who had been at her feet all afternoon, got up from the kitchen floor and walked into the study. He circled once, paused, circled again quietly near the settee, gave a little sigh, and settled into a space on the floor near Henry. He curled up in a calm, resolute sort of comfort, almost as if called.

Ada, drying her hands on a dish towel, stepped cautiously across the floor in her black, tied vinyl pumps, following Chimney from the kitchen and around the corner wall. She saw Henry resting. She stared at him for a long moment.

"Good boy," she whispered to Chimney. She watched another minute as the dog and her brother rested in silence. She noticed a bluebird flutter outside at the horizontal window above, right at the pane.

She went back to the kitchen, poured her toddy into a jar, and set it in the icebox. *Such a luxury*, she thought. An icebox. *Let me see if Jessie is outside at the school crossing.* She walked out the back door and around to the front of the house to the sidewalk and peered over at the drive where the crossing guards always parked. Jessie had finished already and left ... probably took the children home, Ada thought. She would call Jessie on the phone. Ada rarely used a phone. Jessie thought Ada didn't know how to use one.

Jessie received Ada's call and request to come over; she told Heidi to guard the house. Charlotte had run down to Becky's house, and Charles was next door. She could leave for a few minutes. She left the back door open and a note for the children on the counter; then while Ada was dusting and redusting the furniture, opening and then closing and reopening the curtains, Jessie drove the Corvair down Meadow to Main Street and her father.

Inside her old home, below the bedroom where she had slept as a young girl, in the same room where the photograph of her mother had been taken at the lovely window, Jessie walked to her dad on the settee. Staring into her china cabinet in a nervous wait, Ada looked at Jessie in silence, shrugging with a confused expression.

Yes, something was different. The room was different. Jessie carried her dad's mill stool across the room and sat down close to him without disturbing Chimney. Henry turned his head and looked at his daughter.

"Hi, sweet pea," he said.

"Hi, Daddy."

"My life has gotten old," he said with a wry, weak smile. His mouth was dry. "I used to be—"

"So, Daddy," Jessie said, taking her father's hand, "I never asked you. Did you wise men on New Year's Eve decide what time is?"

Henry pulled his set grin into his chest. He looked at his daughter. "It's one hundred pages. Or ... it's God." He swallowed. "Or, it's you. And me."

Henry turned his tired eyes past Jessie's shoulder over to his sister with a look of deep love. Ada felt a panic inside. "Where are the miracles now?" she blurted.

"Want a miracle?" Henry answered slowly, still smiling, his eyes closed. "Go to the garden." He took a small breath. "That's a miracle," he said weakly.

"Daddy," Jessie said gently, "you don't need to talk."

Ada's tears began to fall from her cheek directly to the floor, and she stepped out of the room. In the kitchen, she stood beside a vase of daffodils, wiping her eyes and touching the yellow petals. Jessie held her father's hand more tightly. He was falling into sleep again.

The room grew cold for Jessie. *How odd*, she thought. She pulled her sweater together more tightly. She even shivered a little. "Let me check the thermostat," she began.

"I love you, Jessie," Henry said, calling her to stay, turning his head ever more slowly and barely opening his eyes.

"Are you warm enough?" Jessie asked in fear.

"I love you," he whispered again, closing his eyes. He breathed slowly. "Tell Ethel."

"Yes ... yes," Jessie said, still holding her father's hand. "Daddy. Daddy?" She looked into his face, which looked like that of a young man ... even a little boy.

Jessie recalled how, as a little girl, she had felt fear when her father turned off the lamp on her nightstand and retreated to his own room. The protector was going to sleep.

CHAPTER 11

I t wasn't a perfect painting. The leaves had not been given enough depth with perhaps more dark-green shading. Maybe the artist felt the dance was completed in the flowers. The wild violets in a small arrangement had been painted with good character in eight different hues of purple and blue, twenty-one flowers—no, twenty-three, including the two buds—of happy petals, some crowned in curl to a point, and two of each blossom rounded in skirt. Each blossom was shaded light to dark with a yellow pistil center.

It was the palette of purples—Jessie's favorite color—that she had found calming, satisfying, at the yard sale last year: the purples joined together with delicate brown stems and green spade leaves in a simple earthy vase against a lavender wall, with an interesting backwash of deep, dark plum and a sudden glow of yellow. A lime-ish yellow.

Three days had passed, and Bradford Jones carried the eight-by-ten-inch purple painting, tucked under his arm in a tied cloth bag, into the church and stepped to the pedestal table to sign the guest book near the church entrance for the funeral for Henry Marshall Hall.

The signature lines of the funeral registry pages began to fill. One after another, signatures of dark, thick pencil script with varying loops of heavy lettering took shape.

Mr. and Mrs. J. B. Baker. Mr. and Mrs. Dutton. Ralph Brooks. Merlin Beign. Mr. and Mrs. George Shiller. Edison Harris. Frances and Ruby. Powell. Leskovich. McMillan. Cromwell. Buckner. The Walker family. Virginia Dolman. Once again a car was moving across the map, northeast from Columbus, from Harmony Street, this time with the Wolfe family approaching West Emmette to be with Jessie for the day.

Jessie stared ahead in numbness, in her great loss so soon after her Matthew, barely noticing the faces as they approached her to express love and regret at her father's funeral. She stood between Ada and Ethel. She was letting Ethel speak and react to most of the friends filing by. Jessie didn't want to talk or think. At her side were twenty flower arrangements, and the room smelled heavily of carnations and roses. No petunias. The petunias were at home. There was her dear father, lying in the casket behind her, right there … in a casket. Another casket. All she could hear was, *I love you, Jessie. I love you, Jessie.*

Charles and Charlotte sat in a separated pew in the back left corner of the sanctuary. Grandmother Conrad, Bird, and Ruby were sitting with them. Charles was turning his grandfather's Elgin watch over and over in his pocket, feeling the heavy coolness of the smooth, worn yellow gold. He was reading one of his grandfather's poems printed in the funeral program.

Walter Wolfe walked in short step up to his good friends. Without a word, Charlotte and Charles moved apart on the bench to make room for their Columbus neighbor to sit between them, an old and comfortable habit.

"Henry is with your mother again now, Jessie," someone said softly to Jessie in the receiving line. She nodded. Yes, this was a nice thought. *How does it work?* Jessie wondered again. *Is Daddy with my mother now? Is daddy with her Matthew too? Are they here in this room? Are they here behind us? Or are they far away?* They felt ... far away. Ethel found her sister's hand and grasped it tightly, giving it an urgent squeeze of support.

In came the mayor, the musicians, the Zimmers, Mary Bauer, Paul Coyne, Emmette, Burt Brown, Hazel. And another page of the guest book turned. The friends filled the pews of the small church Henry hadn't belonged to, and others stood in the back. Porter, Winter, Burke, Simms, and Warner and Emma Wolfe. One hundred eighty-two names in solemn pencil later, when the country church could hold no more and the clock struck one, a trumpet and sax began to play a light jazz version of the hymn "In the Garden" from the back of the church. Another trumpet joined in. It was Henry's group. Jessie, Ethel, and Ada sat down in the front pew. Charles and Charlotte were led up front to join them. Walter stayed with them.

A rich spring breeze traveled into the sanctuary through the open church doors, reaching Jessie in her seat. Jessie, pausing to breathe in its scent with closed eyes, felt relief in its fresh touch. At the doorway, the three musicians continued to play as they walked slowly from the entry to the front, where Herman Bedlow, Henry's friend from Pittsburgh, sat at the organ in wait. As the trumpets and sax reached the front of the church, Herman lifted his hands to the organ keys and joined the song, playing along in sweeping finish, then immediately moved in solo performance into the opening cadence of "I Need Thee Every Hour." Herman was an accomplished organist, maybe a little eccentric, and he took the old church organ to its maximum praise and glory. Then the trumpets rejoined him at the chorus. The sax man moved from there into a solo of "My Old Kentucky

Home," which floated sweetly above the hatted heads, many now bowing toward handkerchiefs and tissue, as teardrops fell from Charles's and others' cheeks.

The music came to a rest, and the mayor approached the podium to begin the spoken service with his thoughts of Henry. "This community is pained to share the death of Henry Marshall Hall," he began slowly, "one of our most honored and beloved citizens, who was called away by Him who doeth all things in glory." Cecil Grisby cleared his throat. "If there is one word that describes better than any other the predominating characteristic of his nature, that word is *loyalty*. He was loyal to his friends, loyal to his family, loyal to his country, and loyal to nature and his God. He is now lost to us, but our loss is his eternal gain." Cecil paused again, looking out into the pews at the faces looking for comfort.

"Henry shared with me the Indian version of the twenty-third Psalm," he continued, "which he typed for me once on his Royal typewriter—which we all know was never still. The North American Plains Indians version, interpreted by missionary Isabel Crawford, reads thus: 'The Great Father above, a Shepherd Chief is. I am His and with Him I want not. He throws out to me a rope, and the name of the rope is love, and He draws me to where the grass is green and the water not dangerous, and I eat and lie down and am satisfied. Sometimes my heart is very weak and falls down, but He lifts me up again and draws me into a good road. His name is Wonderful.'"

Cecil Grisby continued, his assembly of papers trembling a little in his aging, sad hands. "'Sometime—it may be very soon, it may be a long, long time—He will draw me into a valley. It is dark there, but I'll be afraid not, for it is in between those mountains that the Shepherd Chief will meet me, and the hunger that I have in my heart all through this life will be satisfied.'" Cecil read more slowly as he reached the end of the Indian psalm, his voice reaching out to his friend. "'These roads that are away ahead will stay with me through this life and after; and afterward, I will go to live in the Big Tepee and sit down with the Shepherd Chief forever.'"

"Amen," Cecil added, stepping down from the pulpit with a glance over at the casket as the small church choir, gathered in their burgundy loft robes, sang softly. Jessie felt great appreciation for her church friends and her father's friends. Charles listened with a broken heart, still clasping his grandfather's pocket watch like it was life, knowing he was now, for sure, the man of the family.

Reverend Burchard stepped forward in a solemn glide to his platform to tell everyone that Henry had left this world during his favorite month. "It's that time of year when winter is at last gone, and summer is just ahead. It is neither too hot, nor too cold. We are still enjoying the last of the spring flowers, and the roses are ready to bloom. The lawn is beautiful and green, and it seems to be always in need of mowing." The congregation chuckled a little.

"As I sat at the breakfast table this morning, I could see three crows scratching among the newly mowed grass, a mother robin was feeding one of her first families of the season, two chipmunks were zigzagging in antics, and a pair of cardinals were building a nest in the wisteria vine at the back door. As I walked out into this wonderland of May," he said, his voice falling deeply onto the name of the month as if it were a soft cushion, "I knew again the proof of God's presence in this rebirth of nature."

Edison Burchard, with no notes or papers, moved to the center of the chancel and turned his prayerful eyes to those of his friends. "And here it is in May that we are gathered together for a death," he said, pausing, "but for the death of someone who lived his life in May."

Shadowed in the corner, on the floor below the crowded floral arrangements, which flocked the front of the sanctuary, were some white clovers and daisies placed in a jelly jar, once again with no card or name attached. Jessie noticed them now and turned her gaze to her daughter, whose eyes were also set on them. Jessie saw Charlotte glance at Walter, who returned her smile shyly, sharing the orphan flowers.

That night, as the steeple bells chimed softly and sweetly into the evening from the Lutheran church on Main Street, Jessie unfolded the letter from her father, written on his lined journal tablet. Henry had told Jessie to take the envelope from his desk drawer that last day, three days ago, explaining that the man who had broken into the house had taken the box with her mother's locks of hair. And now Jessie read her father's artful script, visibly showing a bit more halted and wavering slant.

> Jessie,
> Your mother did not yet know the richness of
> time passing. Like your Matthew, she did not
> have the chance to know the lessons of middle age
> and beyond. A memory is felt differently at age
> thirty, fifty, and then again at seventy. A rifle and
> a clock, a photo, a painting, change dramatically
> in story over time. I was blessed to reach this age.
> Do not be sad for me.

In the days following Henry's funeral, one by one Henry's clocks slowed and stopped their measure of time. Ada and Bird did not wind them with the mornings. Ada told Jessie and Ethel to each take their clocks home, sharing Henry's wishes. Charles was given the Metzger rifle. Charlotte was given the bell from her grandfather's desktop, and she was told she would one day inherit his notebooks. And somewhere the earth rumbled.

It wasn't until October that Jessie decided where to mount her inherited clock, the ornate Gustav Becker regulator, and she asked Gloria next door to ask Luther whether he would help her hang it. He knocked on the door that very evening. Heidi barked and greeted him, her tail wagging. Jessie was at the kitchen table, sewing a button on her coat.

"Where do you want the clock, Jessie?" Luther asked in his booming, sharp voice as he stepped into the kitchen. He was in his carpenter's overalls, as always, with hammer and toolbox in hand.

"Thank you for coming over, Luther," Jessie said, setting down her needle and thread. "I know you work long hours."

"No more than you, darlin'!" he said, looking about.

Jessie stepped over to a wall space in the dinette by the china cabinet. "Here?" she asked, pointing. "Or should it be in the living room, on the paneling?"

"Let's see if we can find a stud." Luther had helped Bill Zimmer build this house. He tapped on the wall doubtfully and looked at the china cabinet, which was full of Jessie's beautiful pink Haviland dinnerware, close by. "Maybe we should look at the living room wall." They went to the right side of the paneled wall, where Luther knew exactly where a stud was, in the seam he had formed when he placed the cherrywood for his newly widowed neighbor. Effortlessly he drew from his box the correct wall screw and mounting, drilled a little, screwed the bolt into the wall, and within a breath was securing the mount on the wall to the stud. Just as swiftly, he lifted the heavy clock, holding it upright, and placed the storied timepiece onto its new throne.

"What's that I smell?" Luther called out over his shoulder. There was a faint burn in the air.

"The pies?" Jessie asked.

"No. A burn."

"Oh, that. Charles is downstairs working on a scout project. He's building a birdhouse and probably using the wood-burning tool," Jessie answered.

"Can I have a look?" Luther asked, placing his tools back in the toolbox.

Thud, thud, thud. Luther's steps in his work boots down the pine basement stairs were heavier than those of the three house occupants combined. Luther found Charles in the back corner of the basement at his father's workbench, a heavy oak plank tabletop set across an old dresser chest.

"Hey, Charles," Luther said. Then, noticing Charlotte nearby, he added, "Hi, sweetheart." Charles tightly gripped the wood-burning pen, which was plugged into the light socket above the bench. Smoke rose from the piece of wood he was working on.

"What are you making?" Luther asked Charles.

"Well, a birdhouse and a picture of a bird," Charles answered. He had drawn a figure in pencil on one of the side panels, not assembled yet, and had burned in short lines one of the stick legs, along with his initials.

"Looks good!" Luther said. "Can I watch you for a minute?"

Charlotte was painting a plastic model on the bench near Charles's project and glanced over as Charles pressed the corded heat pen into the wood and seared a line for the beak.

"Where did you get the wood?" Luther asked.

"The scout leader gave us the kit."

Luther nodded. "Nice piece of pine."

"Yeah," Charles said.

"Well, you're doin' it right," Luther said, watching Charles start the next line. "Just take your time and be careful." He watched another minute. "You might want to lean the burner pen a little more to the left or right to add some size to your ridges."

Charles looked up at the tall man in overalls and nodded. Then he looked down at his bench and tried the other bird leg line like that. It worked. "I like that," he said.

Luther glanced at the instructions and parts sorted on the bench and nodded. "Looks like you're doin' just fine. Just run

over next door with any questions, Charles. Looks fine to me."
He winked at Jessie, who had also come down to see.

Returning up the stairs, Luther said to Jessie, "You be at the
village council meeting Thursday?"

Jessie nodded. Luther continued, "Did you hear? The Lions
Club is gonna create some food baskets for needy families." The
club now had fifteen members. "It would be good to get it in the
paper, 'cause we're gonna need to find out who needs the baskets."

"Okay. Yes, I'll be there. I'll add that to the council report.
I'm not sure that will lead us to the families, but we'll try," Jessie
said.

"Sam Wright said he'll throw in some hams and turkeys."
Sam was the owner of Wright's Grocery. They reached the
kitchen, and Luther added, "Basketball team is lookin' good for
the upcoming season."

"Is it?" Jessie said.

"Might go to state playoffs this year, I'll bet," Luther said, then
added, "Bridg is dating the forward, you know."

"Here, Luther," Jessie said, handing him a cherry pie. "This
is for you and Gloria."

Luther accepted the warm pie with a grateful smile and said
good night.

❊ ❊ ❊

By mid-October, the Lions Club and the township council
of five churches had raised a fund of $210 for the food baskets.
Luther, Paul, Raymond, Mayor Cecil, Sam Wright, Burt Brown,
and Ken Zimmer, the youngest of the Zimmer brothers, called
a meeting at the Lutheran church to plan a date to shop and
assemble the baskets and determine who would receive them.
Jessie also attended the meeting with notepad and with Gloria
Walker, Mrs. Jones, and others.

"We have a problem," Luther said, standing in front of the group. "No one will raise their hand for help. No one answered our flyers."

"Well, ain't that no surprise," Sam said.

"We're gonna have to make a list over the next two weeks," Ken said. "Any of us know who needs help?"

The men in the room turned their heads to the wall or looked down at the floor, thinking. The women whispered to each other. Slowly Raymond Jones raised his hand. "I think McNolty could use a basket."

The room quickly grew silent. No questions asked. Everyone knew the McNolty family and their eight children; they knew they could always use help. The mayor wrote down the name. "Yes, good," he said. "I think that's good."

"How about the Shaw family?"

"Definitely," a number of residents agreed aloud. The men and women stirred in their seats, beginning to feel some excitement and accomplishment.

"How about Jace Field?" someone said. The men nodded slowly.

"Yes," Sam said, and Jace's name was penciled on the paper.

"And that new custodian of the Methodist church," Ken added.

Jessie wasn't put on the list. She was doing all right. In fact, she had just purchased a metronome, and on Saturday morning she was reading the instructions to Charlotte. "See? You set the dial this way." She slid the silver tab to "42," for a slow pace. "Largo," she noted, pointing to the small chart. "The booklet says, 'The metronome serves to denote the tempo at which a musical composition is to be performed. The tempo is specified at the beginning of a composition,' as you know, Charlotte, as Mrs. Bauer has pointed out." Jessie continued reading with novel interest, holding the beautiful contraption in her slender hand.

"'For "80," for example,'" she read, "'the sliding weight on the pendulum is raised until the upper edge of the weight is in exact alignment with the line marked "80" on the scale. Then set the pendulum in motion.'"

Jessie gave the thin, metal shaft a gentle push with her index finger, and the thin rod swung awkwardly left and right in a moderately paced click. Charlotte watched with a frozen expression. Jessie felt pride.

"Try it before Mrs. Bauer arrives. Won't she be surprised?" she said with delight, setting the wooden pillar box on the polished and dust-free piano top. Charlotte tried to match a scale to the slow, loud, slicing click. The metal rod swung oddly back and forth, top heavy with its attached upper slidable weight, like an upside-down clock pendulum. Charlotte's first attempt to play her notes to speed didn't match the clicks, and she tried over again to keep pace.

Jessie went back to the kitchen, glancing at the painting of the violets, the funeral gift from Mr. Jones, which hung on the wall above the telephone stand. It was October 20, and Charles was in the garage, filling a bucket with some garden tools and tulip bulbs, setting them in the car with a rake and shovel for a trip to the cemetery for fall cleanup. When Mary arrived, she brought for Jessie some plant starts for lilies of the valley, and Jessie planted those at the base of the woods during Charlotte's lesson before they left for the cemetery.

Down the road, Simon and Bill were at Bill's kitchen table, studying their expenses from 1962 and planning their course of work for next year's spring. They would open the lake in two more Mays, they figured.

CHAPTER 12

G one were Pigeon and Chase and their card games. Gone were Lake and Minnie Palmer from their lives. Gone were the Wolfes. But Meadow Drive felt good to Jessie. The ground felt like home, she thought, as her third December in West Emmette arrived.

The small pond in the treed grove behind the Catholic church, in front of the newly built rectory, had begun to freeze. Jessie was able to buy Charlotte a Betty Crocker junior cookbook, a nifty file drawer box for her rock collection, and the new Password game. And for Charles, she purchased a new pair of skates and a basketball game in a box. Two weeks before Christmas, Jessie wrapped these presents and placed them on the upper shelf of her closet, in wait of December 25. Sliding the door to a close, she smiled, knowing Charlotte would be sneaking in to peer up at the gift boxes in holiday paper.

This December Charlotte and her mom followed a magazine's directions to make a wreath with tissue paper by molding a coat hanger into a circle and tying cut strips of red, green, and white tissue to the metal until the wire circle held a fat, colorful wreath, which they adorned with a ribbon at the top. They would give the first wreath to Mary.

Most of the cookies had been made—the filled clothespin cookies, the gingerbread men, the sugar cookies with red and green sprinkles, and the peanut butter rounds. The cookies were boxed and stored on the shelves in the garage, which was as cold as a second refrigerator. Most of the holiday cards had been mailed.

On December 20, Meadow Drive was alight at night with electric window candles up and down its riverlike course, where front windows were accented by colorful Christmas trees under roofs edged with icicles growing like glassy grass from young gutters. Snow was dutifully falling, and the street filled once again with sleds and laughter. The street, a new line and curve on the township map, was now well addressed and fully connected by new friends and a generation of neighbors.

Martin McMillan called Jessie on the phone. "You're doing a fine job, Jessie. Listen, I think there is a story in the growth of your village, and I want you to start to think about it," he said.

The anchoring city of Riverton was also growing, with its puffing and rolling steel mills and supporting businesses. The newspaper was celebrating a new plant and editorial offices on Federal Street, and the scouts of Troop Four, from West Emmette and Clover Township, received a tour of the printing plant on December 27. The newspaper reported, "With teletype machines bringing news from all over the world, type-setting machines turning news copy into print, and giant presses sending forth hundreds of newspapers per minute, today's visitors saw a great newspaper in the making." The front-page article continued with a list of the visitors' names, which began with Jackie Walker and included Charles Conrad, Bobby Braunhall, Sebastian Bowmaster,

Mitch Simmons, Stevie West, and twenty more, including Mr. McMillan's own two children.

That night while Jessie and Charlotte folded kitchen towels at the table, Jessie thought of Uncle Perry in Florida and his October 1960 letter of love and concern. She thought of Pigeon in Cleveland and of Warner and Emma and Walter and their Columbus friends and how she missed them all. Her former life of dinners, using their beautiful china and gold-leafed crystal glasses, floated behind her in the oak china cabinet Matthew had made. Her former life had already moved behind glass, set away on the shelves.

The Holy Bible she had been given upon Matthew's burial was the King James Version with an antique white, embossed cover, with "pages edged in gold," so the label read. The box it came in was covered in a crinkled, silver paper that resembled Christmas wrapping. As sympathy cards had arrived during the blurry days and weeks that followed that dark October day in 1960, just over two years ago, Jessie had placed the cards in the box, for she kept the Bible at her bedside. The box had filled with prayers and floral cards and four-cent stamps. She glanced again at the top envelope, looked briefly at Emma's letter with its pretty white rose stationery, then placed the box in the left side of her china cabinet and latched the glass door.

That night on Harmony Street in Columbus, Walter was painting a model car, a new Dodge, wishing he could show it to Charles. There still weren't any other boys on the street, except for one he didn't like. No longer interested in Scouts, he was more often tagging along with his dad. Maybe he would try ball in the spring. Or just help his dad with the garden. And he did like to read and to work in the yard.

Under the December moons in West Emmette, as the air iced into frozen glitter, inch by inch by inch the water of Father's Pond, as it was called, had frozen into a solid surface of skateable glass. Mr.

Bowmaster and two of his street neighbors helped Father Parker scrape the new ice with their shovels, clearing the fallen snow with long, scratching pushes and heaving throws of snow, their jacketed arms swinging back and forth, back and forth, while they checked each step of the new surface with their boots for safety.

Under the December half-moon, Ben Bowmaster thought to create a fire pit at the corner of the pond, where there was a grated drain and several boulders. He and the priest pulled together a few extra stones to form some seats and stacked some firewood. One by one by two by four, children and some parents came to the ice to skate, including Jessie, Charles, and Charlotte. By late January, parents were confident enough to stay at home, and nights at the pond held only the children of town, where the boys did the shoveling and played hockey and Fox and Geese, and tried to keep the girls at bay.

Father Parker watched them from his window. So did Mrs. Trunke across Field Street and Mrs. Bowmaster across the lawn. Blades razored from the pond's edge onto the lake surface, onto the rough ice that held Charles and Charlotte up for whichever way they chose to turn, while at 147 Jessie listened to the waltzing Perry Como recording of "When You Come to the End of the Day" playing on the hi-fi radio.

It was a joyous flurry of hats and scarves and scrapes and whacks of the pucks and laughter at the pond. The pushed-up snow, the shoveled mounds of it, was second nature to the children, as though winter were fashioned for them. It wasn't cold, and it was. The happy shedding of snow- and ice-layered coats and mittens was just a natural part of the day's end. It was never dark in the winter at the pond. The white lawn banked up around the children, and the winter sky was a glowing blue. The evening or morning was part of a cycle—not day or night but a time for skating or a time to race bicycles in the woods or a time for ball or berry picking.

The Gustav Becker clock on the living room wall provided a peaceful pace for the Conrads, and soon the young 1963 calendar was turned to February. Jessie saw joy in the valentines her children received in school and from Mary Bauer and Bridget Walker. A valentine even arrived in the mail to Charlotte from Walter, which surprised Jessie, who, leaning into her daughter's bedroom door that evening to say good night, caught sight of Charlotte reaching into the pink jewelry box. She saw Charlotte take the pink rhinestone ring from the top center slot of felt and place it on her left-hand finger. Charlotte gently closed the lid and stepped into a few balancé ballet glides. She did a pretty glissade and another, then a soutenu turn; then she slowly leaned into a graceful, dramatic, dreamlike bow.

Silently Jessie stepped back from the door, closing it quietly with a loving smile. Charlotte's cat was at her feet. Jessie picked up the young cat with a tender hug, walked to her desk, and took from the drawer a new notebook of paper. She felt satisfied with the decisions she had made and, like her father, would begin a journal of thoughts and observations, especially for Charles and Charlotte.

The End

I wish, I wish I could go back to the pond tonight, right now, just one more night, and step upon the rough, whitened glass again—where we were together yet so beautifully alone with our growing selves, with our youth, where the only anchor was the blade on the bottom of the skate.

ABOUT THE AUTHOR

J. Penrod Scott, who grew up in Ohio and studied English literature, has worked as a journalist for a national magazine and as a corporate writer and publishes a family board game. Scott is grateful for a loving family, wonderful friends, and a great brother.